EX LIBRIS

VINTAGE CLASSICS

JOURNEY TO THE CENTRE
OF THE EARTH

Jules Verne was born on 8 February, 1828, in the city of Nantes, France. He is best known for his novels *Journey to the Centre of the Earth*, *Twenty Thousand Leagues Under the Sea*, *The Mysterious Island* and *Around the World in Eighty Days*. Verne is often referred to as the 'father of science fiction' because he wrote about space, air and underwater travel before aeroplanes, spacecrafts and submarines were invented. He died in 1905.

OTHER WORKS BY JULES VERNE

JULES VERNE

Journey to the Centre of the Earth

TRANSLATED FROM THE FRENCH BY
Joyce Gard

VINTAGE BOOKS
London

Published by Vintage 2011

8 10 9

Journey to Centre of the Earth was first published in France as
Voyage au centre de la terre in 1864

This edition first published by Hutchinson in 1961

Vintage
Random House, 20 Vauxhall Bridge Road,
London SW1V 2SA

www.vintage-classics.info

Addresses for companies within The Random House Group Limited
can be found at: www.randomhouse.co.uk/offices.htm

The Random House Group Limited Reg. No. 954009

A CIP catalogue record for this book
is available from the British Library

ISBN 9780099528494

Penguin Random House is committed to a sustainable future for
our business, our readers and our planet. This book is made from
Forest Stewardship Council® certified paper.

MIX
Paper from
responsible sources
FSC® C018179

Printed and bound in Great Britain by Clays Ltd, St Ives plc

Contents

Journey to the Centre
of the Earth

1

My Uncle Finds a Manuscript

On Sunday, 24th May, 1863, my uncle Professor Lidenbrock came suddenly home, much too early for dinner. I was in the dining-room of our house, No. 19 Königstrasse, in the old quarter of Hamburg, when I caught a glimpse of him dashing along the street, and at the same time our housekeeper Martha put her head round the door.

'Here's the master already!' she cried, 'and I've only just got the dinner in the oven!'

'Never mind, Martha,' I said soothingly, 'he has no right to expect his dinner yet.' But in my heart I felt that if my uncle were hungry nothing would stop him from shouting for his food the moment he set foot in the house.

'Then why is he home so early? Here he is, I'll get back to my kitchen, do please calm him down, Mr Axel.'

When she had gone, however, I thought it would be more prudent to avoid my violent uncle. I was just going to sneak upstairs to my little room when the street door creaked on its hinges, the wooden staircase echoed with heavy footsteps, and the master of the house rushed through the dining-room on the way to his study. As he passed, he flung his walking-stick with its nutcracker head into a corner, his broad, tousle-haired hat on to the table, and shouted in ringing tones, 'Axel, follow me!'

Before I had time to move he was calling impatiently:

'Well, where are you, boy?'

I ran into the study. My uncle Otto Lidenbrock was not unkind, only terribly eccentric. He was a true scientist, and although he sometimes broke his specimens through testing them too abruptly, he was a brilliant geologist and mineralogist.

He was tall and thin, fair-haired, with an iron constitution, looking ten years younger than his age, which was about fifty. His eyes behind his big spectacles were always glancing eagerly about, his long thin nose was like a filed blade, and unkind people said that it was magnetic and attracted iron filings. That was untrue, it only attracted large quantities of snuff. He walked with enormous strides, and always with clenched fists, which is supposed to be the sign of an impulsive nature.

For a German professor he was fairly rich. He owned his house and all that was in it. His household consisted of his god-daughter Gretel – a girl of seventeen – the housekeeper Martha, and myself. As I was his nephew and also an orphan, I became his laboratory assistant. This delighted me because I was passionately interested in geology and had the blood of a mineralogist in my veins.

In spite of my uncle's fiercely impatient nature, I was happy, because he was very fond of me. But he did not know how to wait. When in April he planted mignonette and morning-glory in pots on the drawing-room window-sill, he went every day regularly to pull them by the leaves to make them grow faster.

He was certainly not a man to put up with disobedience,

and so when he called me I hurried into his study. I found him deep in his large plush armchair, holding a book in his hands and turning over the pages with delighted admiration.

'What a book! What a treasure!' he cried. My uncle was a lover of rare books, and spent his idle moments rummaging in the second-hand bookstalls.

'What book is it?' I asked, trying to sound as if I really cared.

'Why, it's the *Heimskringla* of Snorri Sturlusson, the famous Icelandic author of the twelfth century; it is the Chronicle of the Norwegian princes who ruled in Iceland!'

'Is it finely printed?' I asked.

'*Print!* My dear boy, it's not *print*, it's a manuscript, a runic manuscript!'

'Runic?'

'Yes, runic – I suppose you don't know what runes are? I'll explain – they are an ancient form of writing supposed to have been invented by Odin, the Father of the Gods, himself.'

I was trying to think of something suitable to say, when suddenly a greasy parchment slipped out of the book and glided to the floor. My uncle fell upon it with an excited cry and unfolded it carefully on the table. The parchment was five inches long by three inches wide, covered with lines of cabbalistic writing. I will copy them exactly, because they were the cause of sending us off on the strangest expedition of the nineteenth century:

```
ᛩ.ᛡᚴᛑᚱᛘ    ᛏ�759ᚴᚾᛏᛑ    ᛘᛏᛂᚱᛁᛒᛑ
ᛘᛃᛏ�424ᛃᚨ    ᚾᚴᛏᛂᛁᛏᚨ    ᚴᛁᛏᛒᛡᚱᛏ
ᚱᛏ,4ᛁᛃᛑ    ᛁᛏᚴᛁᛏᛏᛂ    ᚤᚾ ᛂᛒᛡᚴᚴ
ᛏᛃᛏᛡᛁᛏᛁ    ᚴᚾᛏᛃᛃᚱᛏ    ᚴᚴᛁ ᛁᚤᛁ
ᛁᛏᚾᛁᛁᚴ    .ᚴᛝᚤᛡᚤ    ᛁᛏᛁᛁᛒᛃ
ᚤᚤᛒᚴᛂᛁ    ᛏᛏᚾᛏᚾᛂ    ᚠᚴᛁᚴᛏᚾ
ᛒᛏ、ᛁᛏᛂ    ᛂᛃᛏᛁᛒᛂ    ᚤᛏᛒᛁᛁᛁ
```

5

The professor brooded for a long time over these outlandish signs, then he pushed up his glasses and said:

'It's certainly runic, the characters are just the same as in the manuscript. But what can they mean? Surely the language must be ancient Icelandic?'

I must say I was rather pleased to see my uncle mystified, because he was supposed to know most of the languages of the world. However, he was naturally irritated because he did not immediately understand the writing, and I was preparing for a violent scene, when the study door opened and Martha announced that the soup was on the table.

'To hell with the soup!' he cried, 'and with you too!'

Martha fled, I followed her and took my place at the dinner table. I waited for a few minutes, but the professor did not come. It was certainly very unlike him to miss dinner. And what a dinner! Parsley soup, a ham omelette spiced with sorrel and nutmeg, a loin of veal with plum sauce, and for dessert, sugared prawns, all washed down with a good Moselle wine. That is what my uncle's old piece of paper cost him. But I made up for his loss, like a devoted nephew. I was just munching my last prawn when he started shouting for me, and I hurried back into the study.

2

Saknussemm's Cryptogram

'It's certainly runic,' said the professor with a frown. 'But there's a secret, and I'm going to find it out, or else!' He waved his arms fiercely. 'Sit there,' he went on, pointing with his fist, 'and write.' I sat down at the table. 'Now, I'm going to dictate to you each letter of our alphabet which corresponds to each one of these Icelandic characters, and we'll see what we get. Mind you don't make any mistakes!'

He called out the letters and I wrote them down, and soon we had the following nonsensical words:

mm.rnlls	esreuel	seecJde
sgtssmf	unteief	niedrke
kt,samn	atrateS	Saodrrn
emtnael	nuaect	rrilSa
Atvaar	.nscrc	ieaabs
ccdrmi	eeutul	frantu
dt,iac	oseibo	KediiY

When I had finished my uncle snatched the paper and studied it carefully for a long time.

'What can it mean? It must be a cipher. When I think that some great discovery must be hidden here!' He was almost beside himself with frustration. Then he took up the book and the parchment and compared them carefully.

'The writings are not in the same hand,' he said. 'The cipher is later than the book. I'll tell you how I know: the first letter is a double *m* which only came into the Icelandic alphabet in the fourteenth century. Therefore there must be at least two hundred years between the manuscript and the document.'

I saw his point.

'That leads me to suppose,' my uncle went on, 'that one of the owners of the book must have drawn these mysterious characters. I wonder if he signed his name somewhere in the manuscript?'

He pushed up his spectacles and took a strong reading-glass, then began to examine the first pages of the book. On the back of the fly-leaf he discovered a sort of blotch, looking like an ink-stain. He examined it closely and at last managed to make out some faint runic characters, which I will copy:

ᛏᛣᚾᛐ   ᛋᛏᚱᛣᚦᛋᛋᛏᛪ

'Arne Saknussemm!' he cried triumphantly. 'I know that name! He was an Icelandic scholar of the sixteenth century, a famous alchemist.'

Even I was beginning to be excited now.

'These alchemists, like Roger Bacon and Paracelsus, were the only real scientists of their time; they made the most astonishing discoveries. Now I wonder what Saknussemm wanted to conceal in this cipher – what fantastic invention? I'll find out. I'll crack his code, I'll tear out his secret, I'll neither eat nor sleep till I've mastered this document!' My heart sank. 'And that goes for you too, Axel!' I was glad I had done so well at dinner.

'Now first of all,' my uncle went on, 'what is the language of this cipher? It can't be too difficult. There are one hundred and thirty-two letters in the document, with seventy-nine consonants and fifty-three vowels. The languages of Southern Europe are made up in about those proportions, while those of the North are very much richer in consonants. Now what language, do you think?' I waited for him to go on.

'Saknussemm was a learned man, and if he wasn't writing in his mother tongue he would be almost bound to use the common language of scholars, that is to say, Latin. If that doesn't work out, I'll try Spanish, French, Italian, Greek and Hebrew. But I'm almost certain that it will turn out to be Latin.'

'That stuff?' I said. 'It doesn't look like Latin to me.'

'Yes, Latin,' said my uncle, 'but scrambled Latin.'

If you unscramble that, I was thinking, I'll give you full marks.

'The words are all jumbled up,' he went on, 'but there must be a key. Axel, can you find the key?'

I hardly heard his question, I was day-dreaming. My eyes had been caught by Gretel's picture on the wall. She was away staying with relations at Altona, and I missed her very much;

she and I were in love and had become secretly engaged. My uncle had no suspicions, he was sunk in his geology and had forgotten what it was like to be young. Gretel was a lovely blonde with blue eyes, rather a serious girl, and we were very much in love.

My uncle roused me by banging the table with his fist.

'Now attend to me!' he said. 'The most obvious way of mixing up the letters of a sentence is to write the words vertically instead of horizontally. Let's see what happens. Axel, write a sentence on this piece of paper – any sentence – but write it downwards in columns, in groups of five or six letters.'

I saw what he meant and at once I wrote, from the top downwards:

```
I       y       y       i       e
l       o       d       n       t
o       u       a       g       e
V       ,       r       G       l
e       m       l       r
```

Good,' said the professor. 'Now write those letters out like words along one line.' This was the result:

Iyyie   lodnt   ouage   v,rGl   emlr

'Fine!' said my uncle, snatching the paper from my hands. 'That begins to look like the old parchment – vowels and consonants in strange disorder, capitals and commas in the middle of words. Now all I have to do to read your sentence is to take the first letter of each word, then the second, and so

10

on.' And then, to his great surprise and also to mine, he read:

'I love you, my darling Gretel.'

I had given myself away in my thoughtlessness.

'Well, well, so you love Gretel!' said my uncle in a stern voice.

'Yes . . . that is, no . . .' I stammered in confusion.

'Well, well, you love Gretel,' he went on mechanically. 'Well now, let's try the same thing with the document!' He had already forgotten my foolish words. He took up the parchment with a trembling hand, in great excitement. Then he cleared his throat, and taking the first letter of each word, then the second, he dictated the following series:

> *mmessunkaSenrA.icefdoK.segnittamurtn*
> *ecertserrette,rotaivsadua,ednecsedsadne*
> *lacartniiiluJsirtracSarbmutabiledmek*
> *meretarcsilucoYsleffenSnI*

As I took down the letters they meant nothing to me, of course, but I hoped that when I had finished the professor would roll out a magnificent Latin sentence. But instead he banged the table, the ink spurted, the pen flew out of my hands.

'It's all wrong!' he shouted. 'There's not an atom of sense in it!' He shot out of the study like a bullet, rushed down the stairs like an avalanche, flung himself into the street and made off like a whirlwind.

3

The Key to the Cipher

When he had gone I began classifying a collection of geodes, those hollow stones lined with little crystals, which a French mineralogist had just sent us. I sorted and labelled them and arranged them in a glass case, but all the time I was thinking about the old document. I was troubled by a strange anxiety; I felt that some catastrophe was hanging over us.

After an hour or so I had finished arranging the stones. I sank down at ease in the big armchair and lit my pipe. This pipe had a long curved stem and a bowl carved in the form of a graceful nymph: little by little she was burning black and changing into a negress. I listened for my uncle's step on the stair, but all was quiet. I wondered where he could be and imagined him dashing along under the trees of the country road, running his stick along the wall, punishing the grasses, beheading the thistles and disturbing the solitary storks.

I was wondering whether he would return triumphant or discouraged, whether the riddle would beat him or he the riddle, and all the time I was holding idly in my hands the paper on which I had written down that series of incomprehensible letters.

What can it all mean? I was thinking. I began trying to make sense out of the letters, and first I tried grouping them in twos, and threes, and fives, and sixes. But that was no good. Then I noticed that certain words could indeed be discovered – for example the English words 'ice' and 'sir', the Latin 'mutabile' and 'ira' the French 'mer' and 'mère'. But these words seemed to have been formed purely by chance and I did not feel I was on the right track.

I was beginning to grow dizzy through studying these one hundred and thirty-two letters so long. They seemed to be floating round my head, as if they had got loose from the paper and were buzzing about like a swarm of bees. I felt I was suffocating and began automatically to fan myself with the sheet of paper.

And then, as I waved the paper, with sometimes the front and sometimes the back towards me, it seemed that words were forming before my eyes – Latin words, quite easy to read. I caught the word 'craterem' and then 'terrestre'.

Suddenly I saw light. I had discovered the key to the cipher. The professor had been perfectly correct in his guesses, both as to the arrangement of the letters and the language of the document. Only one little piece had been missing from the jigsaw, and now I had stumbled by chance on that missing clue!

I was overcome by excitement, my eyes were swimming so that I could not see. I laid the sheet of paper on the table and walked twice round the room to steady my nerves, then I sank down into the enormous armchair.

At last I took a deep breath and said to myself, 'Read!'

I stood up and leaned over the table, and putting my finger

under each letter in turn, I read the sentence through without a pause.

I was struck with terror. That a man should have dared such a deed!

I uttered a wild cry. 'No! No! My uncle must never know! Nothing would stop him from following in this man's footsteps, from attempting this desperate journey! And he'd drag me with him, and we should never come back! Never! Never!' I was almost fainting with fear. Then a thought struck me. 'I must destroy the paper at once, before he can stumble on the solution.'

There was still a little fire in the grate. I snatched up not only the sheet of paper, but also Saknussemm's original parchment. I was just going to throw them on the coals and wipe out this dangerous secret for ever, when the study door opened and my uncle appeared.

4

I Have Doubts

I put the paper back hastily on the table, but Professor Lidenbrock had noticed nothing, he was deep in thought.

He sat down in his armchair and, pen in hand, began working out permutations and combinations according to some mathematical formula which he must have thought out during his walk. I watched his trembling hand as he wrote. My own nerves were keyed up to fever pitch by my secret knowledge.

For three hours he worked without speaking or raising his head, endlessly scratching out and beginning again. Night fell, the street-sounds were hushed, my uncle was still bent over his task. He neither saw nor heard Martha when she put her head round the door to ask him if he would take supper. At last I was overcome by drowsiness and fell asleep on the sofa.

When I awoke next morning he was still at work. I could see by his red-rimmed eyes and haggard look, his tousled hair and feverish cheeks, that he had not slept a wink. I was sorry for him, and when I gently reproached him he was not even angry with me. All his energy was concentrated on his single purpose so that I felt he would blow up like a blocked volcano. By one word I could loosen the steel vice which bound his brain. But I did not speak.

'No, no!' I thought to myself. 'I know him too well; if I tell him there'll be no holding him back. I should be signing his death-warrant if I were to tell him the secret.' So I sat back with folded arms.

But I was reckoning without the professor's peculiarities. When Martha wanted to go to market she found the street door locked and the key missing. My uncle had evidently taken away the key, either by accident or design, when he came back from his walk the evening before.

'So that's it, is it,' I thought. 'Martha and I are to die of hunger, we are to be the innocent victims of his crazy notions.'

I remembered an occasion a few years back, when my uncle had been working at his great mineralogical classification. He had gone without food for forty-eight hours, and all the household had had to do likewise. I had a good healthy appetite and I still remembered my pangs of hunger.

Now it looked as if there would be no dinner today, as there had been no supper the night before. I made up my mind to bear it stoically, but Martha was very doleful. My uncle was still at work. He was in a world of his own, far above the earth, and evidently he had no need of earthly nourishment.

But it was different with us. Towards midday I grew almost desperate with hunger. Martha had innocently eaten up everything in the larder the night before, and there was nothing in the house. However, I decided to stick it out as a point of honour.

The clock struck two. My resolution was weakening, the whole affair began to appear slightly ridiculous. My uncle would surely never believe the document, or if he did, he could be forcibly prevented from following in Saknussemm's footsteps. Anyway, he might discover the key to the cipher for himself at any moment, and then all my sufferings would have been in vain.

Now I thought how foolish I had been to wait for so long. I was working out some means of breaking it gently when the professor got to his feet, took his hat, and made ready to go out. So he was going out and leaving us still locked in! It was the last straw.

'Uncle!' I said. He took no notice.

'Uncle Otto!' I called in a louder voice.

'What?' he muttered, like a man suddenly roused from sleep.

'The key . . .'

'What key? The door-key?'

'No,' I said, 'the key of the document.'

The professor looked at me over the top of his glasses; he must have seen something in my face, because he gripped my arm. His question was silent but none the less clear to my mind.

I nodded. He shook his head sorrowfully, as if I were mad. I nodded again, very definitely. His eyes darted fire, his grip on my arm was fierce. It was the strangest conversation, held entirely in silence, and indeed I hardly dared utter a word; I was terrified that my uncle would hug me to death like a bear in the transport of his joy. But he gripped me so violently that at last I was forced to answer.

'Yes, the key . . . quite by chance . . .'

'Well? Well?' He was bursting with excitement.

'Here,' I said, giving him the piece of paper on which I had written, 'read.'

'But it's nonsense!' He crumpled the paper angrily.

'Nonsense if you begin at the beginning – but try beginning at the end . . .' My words were cut short by a bellow from the professor as he saw light. He flung himself on the paper, smoothing it with a trembling hand, and read out the whole document from the last letter to the first in a voice which shook with emotion. This was the message:

> *'In Sneffels Yoculis craterem kem delibat*
> *umbra Scartaris Julii intra calendas descende,*
> *audas viator, et terrestre centrum attinges.*
> *Kod feci. Arne Saknussemm.'*

This dog-Latin can be translated as follows:

'Go down into the crater of Snaefells Jökull which the shadow of Scartaris caresses before the kalends of July, bold traveller, and you will reach the centre of the earth. This I have done. Arne Saknussemm.'

My uncle leapt as if from an electric shock; his delight knew no bounds; he walked up and down, holding his head in his hands; he pushed the chairs about and made castles of his books; he even juggled with his precious mineral specimens. At last he calmed down a little and sank into his armchair.

'What's the time?' he said.

'Three o'clock.'

'Past dinner time! I'm dying of hunger. Let's eat. After that . . .'

'After that?'

'You'll pack my box! And yours too!' And he dashed into the dining-room.

5

I Argue with my Uncle

At my uncle's words a shudder passed through my whole body. To go to the centre of the earth! What madness! But I said nothing. I decided to wait till he was calmer and then discourage him by scientific arguments.

He was naturally furious when he found there was no dinner, though it was his own fault. But soon he had set Martha at liberty and she was running to market, and it was not long before we were sitting down to a well-covered table. My uncle was very gay during the meal and even made some of his heavy professorial jokes. As soon as my hunger was satisfied I began thinking out the best way of tackling him.

When we had finished he led the way into the study and sat down at one end of the work-table, while I took my place at the other.

'Axel,' he said, beaming at me, 'you're a clever boy, you've done me a great service. I had almost come to the end of my tether. I'll never forget it, and you shall share my glory.'

Glory, I thought to myself. Well, now he's in a good mood, now's the time.

'But not a word to a soul!' he went on. 'If a murmur of this should reach the outside world, a whole army of rival geologists would be falling over themselves to follow Arne Saknussemm!'

'Do you really think so, Uncle?' I asked. 'How do you know this document isn't a fake?'

'A fake! Think of the book where we found it!'

'Oh, I agree that it was certainly written by Saknussemm himself, but how do you know it wasn't a sort of scientific practical joke?'

At this the professor nearly flew off the handle. But he controlled himself and replied, with a half-smile:

'Well, we shall see.'

I was rather annoyed. 'Well, Uncle, I have a few objections, anyway. May I tell you what they are?'

'Certainly,' he said, with a generous wave of his arm. 'Go right ahead, dear boy. You are no longer my nephew, but my colleague.'

'First of all, then, I should like to know what these names mean – Jökull, Snaefells, Scartaris?'

'Nothing could be easier. Fetch the third atlas in the second section of the large bookcase, series Z, shelf 4.'

I fetched the atlas. My uncle opened it and said:

'This is one of the best maps of Iceland.' I leaned forward to look. 'The island is composed of volcanoes,' he went on, 'and they are all called "Jökull". That is the Icelandic word for glacier, and in that high latitude most of the volcanoes erupt through caps of ice.'

'What about Snaefells?' I asked.

'Look at the west coast. Here is the capital, Reykjavik. Now follow the coastline, bitten by the sea into innumerable fjords, to the north-west, and stop just below the sixty-fifth degree of latitude. What can you see?'

'A sort of peninsula like a bare bone, ending in a huge knee-cap.'

'Yes, that's right, now what is there on that knee-cap?'

'A mountain which seems to have grown up out of the sea.'

'That's Snaefells, a most remarkable mountain, five thousand feet high, and it will certainly be the most famous mountain in the world, if its crater leads to the centre of the globe.'

'But that's impossible!' I said. 'It must be choked up with lava and burning rocks . . .'

'But it's extinct, it hasn't erupted since 1219.'

One of my hopes was dashed. 'But what about Scartaris,' I asked, 'and the kalends of July?'

My uncle reflected for a few moments, then went on: 'This proves the remarkable ingenuity of Saknussemm. Snaefells has several craters, so he had to make clear which he meant. He had noticed that towards the kalends of July, that is about the last days of June, the shadow of one of the peaks of the mountain Scartaris falls on the mouth of the crater in question. What could be a better guide?'

He had an answer to everything. I shifted my ground and began attacking him with more scientific objections.

'All right,' I said, 'I agree that this is a genuine document, and that Saknussemm must have been to Snaefells himself and noticed how the shadow of Scartaris pointed to a certain crater. I suppose there was a local legend about this crater, how it led to the centre of the earth, but I will never believe that he made the journey himself and came back alive to tell the tale.'

'And why not?' said my uncle in a mocking voice.

'Because all scientific theories prove that such a venture is impossible.'

'Theories!' said my uncle. 'Who cares for theories?'

He was making fun of me, but I went on: 'It is well known that the temperature rises by about one degree centigrade for every seventy feet downwards. As the radius of the earth is over four thousand miles, then it follows that the temperature in the centre is about two million degrees. That means that all matter must be in a state of incandescent gas, for nothing can resist such a temperature.'

'You're afraid of the heat, Axel? You don't want to be melted?'

'It's up to you,' I answered crossly.

'Then listen to me,' he said in a superior tone of voice, 'no one has any idea of what goes on down there. Man has not penetrated more than a minute fraction of the distance, and scientific theories are constantly changing as new evidence comes to light. If it were really as hot as all that in the centre, then the whole earth would blow up. But it doesn't; and it looks, too, as if the earth may be cooling down, since there are certainly fewer active volcanoes now than there were in the beginning of the world.'

My uncle was a most persuasive man. As usual, I found I was falling under the influence of his enthusiasm.

'You see, Axel,' he went on in his most charming style, 'there is really not the slightest evidence for an internal furnace, and personally I don't believe it exists. But we'll see for ourselves.'

'Well,' I said grudgingly, 'we'll see then – that is, if we can see anything at all.'

'Why not?' he said. 'There will certainly be some form of electricity in the air, and even the atmosphere may become luminous as we draw near to the centre. But not a word! We don't want anyone else to get there first.'

6

Preparations for the Journey

I walked out of my uncle's study in a daze. I felt I needed air, a great deal of air, and soon I was wandering along the banks of the river Elbe, deep in thought. If we could have set off at that very minute, I would have gone without a qualm, but after an hour or so I had sunk into the depths of depression.

'It's a monstrous suggestion!' I said to myself. 'My uncle can't have been serious.' Then I began to think that it must all have been a bad dream.

I had been walking for a long time and found myself at last on the Altona road. Something must have led me there, for all at once I caught sight of Gretel walking briskly towards me on her way home.

'Gretel!' I called. She looked up in amazement.

'Axel!' she said, 'you've come to meet me! How sweet of you! But what's the matter? You look very odd.'

'You may well ask,' I said, and explained. For a few moments she was silent, and we walked on hand in hand.

'Axel,' she said at last.

'Well, Gretel?'

'It'll be a wonderful trip.' That was a shock! 'Yes, indeed, Axel, and worthy of a professor's nephew. A brave, splendid thing to do, an adventure fit for a man!'

'Why, Gretel, I thought you'd be sure to try and stop me!'

'No, certainly not, Axel darling, and I wish I could come too, but I suppose I'd only be in the way.'

'You mean that?'

'Of course I do,' she said.

Women really are extraordinary creatures, and I didn't quite know how to take this. However, I made one last try.

'I wonder if you'll feel that way tomorrow?' I said.

'But of course, Axel – why not?'

It was dark when we arrived home. I thought we should find everything quiet and peaceful and my uncle already in bed. But the house was in an uproar, the professor was surrounded by a gang of delivery men unloading all sorts of goods and the old housekeeper did not know which way to turn.

'Wherever have you been, Axel?' my uncle called out as soon as he caught sight of me. 'Your box not packed, and my papers not in order, and the key of my travelling-bag missing, and my gaiters not here yet!'

'You mean . . . we're really going?' I could hardly utter the words.

'But of course we're going! And you have to take yourself off for a walk, wretched boy!'

'When do we start?' I muttered.

'The day after tomorrow, at crack of dawn.'

I picked my way through piles of equipment cluttering the passage – rope ladders, flash-lamps, water-bottles, iron crampons, picks, steel-pointed sticks, ice-axes – and made my way miserably upstairs to my room.

I spent a dreadful night. Early next morning someone knocked at my door. I pretended to be still asleep, but Gretel's voice called 'Axel dear!' so I dragged myself out of bed.

I could still not believe in my fate, and I made her come with me to the professor's study.

'Uncle, are we really going?'

'But of course!'

'Well, what's the hurry, then?'

'Time! Time flying! Time the great enemy!'

'But it's only the twenty-sixth of May . . .'

'Idiot! Do you think it's so easy to get to Iceland? If you hadn't rushed off yesterday like a madman, I would have taken you to the shipping office, and you'd realise that there's only one regular service between Copenhagen and Reykjavik, on the twenty-second of each month.'

'Well?'

'If we wait till the twenty-second of June, we shall arrive too late to see the shadow of Scartaris touch the crater of Snaefells, and so we must get to Copenhagen without any more delay and see if we can pick up some small vessel. Go and get packed!'

I went upstairs with a heavy heart. Gretel followed me and packed my bag, cheering me up as best she could.

When the bag was strapped up I went downstairs. All that day more supplies kept coming in: physical apparatus, firearms, electrical equipment. Martha was distracted.

'Is the master out of his mind?' she asked.

I nodded.

'And he's carrying you off with him?'

I nodded again.

'But where are you going?' she wanted to know.

I pointed to the centre of the earth.

'To the cellar, then?' said the old woman.

'Much, much deeper than that, Martha dear.'

At last the evening came. Time was passing as in a dream.

'Tomorrow morning, at six o'clock precisely, we leave the house,' said my uncle.

At ten o'clock I fell into bed like a log. During the night my terrors revived and I had hideous nightmares. I dreamed I was plunging into the abyss, dragged down by the professor's powerful arms. My body was falling ceaselessly, interminably, down unfathomable precipices, gathering momentum as it spun in the sickening gulf.

At five o'clock I woke with a splitting head and ragged nerves. I went down into the dining-room and found my uncle at breakfast, making a hearty meal. I looked at him in disgust, but Gretel was there, and I was silent. All the same, I found I could eat nothing.

At half past five a huge carriage came rumbling along outside and stopped at the house. It was soon loaded up with the equipment for the expedition.

'Where's your luggage?' said my uncle. 'Hurry up with it, or you'll make us miss the train!'

I went upstairs. My fate was sealed, then. Recklessly I shoved my case over the top stair and let it slide bumping down to the bottom. I followed in its wake.

My uncle was solemnly entrusting the house to Gretel's care.

She kissed her guardian and then me. We clung together for a moment.

'Gretel!' I whispered, holding her tight.

'Goodbye, Axel darling,' she murmured. 'I'll be waiting for you, never fear.'

We climbed into the carriage. Martha and Gretel stood on the doorstep, waving, the coachman whipped up the horses, and we set off at a smart gallop towards Altona station.

7

No Head for Heights

Three days afterwards, at ten o'clock in the morning, we set foot in Copenhagen; our baggage was loaded on to a carriage and we drove off to the Phoenix Hotel. We snatched a hasty wash and brush-up, then set out at once to look for a ship.

My last hopes faded when we discovered a small Danish schooner, the *Valkyrie*, due to sail for Reykjavik on 2nd June. Captain Bjarne was on board, and his would-be passenger nearly pumped his hand off in his joy. The captain was somewhat startled by my uncle's enthusiasm; he himself thought nothing of the voyage to Iceland, it was all in the day's work. He took advantage of the professor's excitement to make us pay double fare.

'Come aboard on Tuesday, at seven in the morning,' said the captain, pocketing a nice fat wad of banknotes. We walked back to the hotel.

'This is wonderful,' said my uncle, rubbing his hands. 'What fantastic luck! Everything is going our way! Now let's have a bite of lunch, then we'll explore the town.'

We found a French restaurant where we had an excellent

lunch at a very reasonable price, then strolled about the city, looking at the sights as tourists do. I wished so much that my sweetheart could be there, and found myself miserably wondering whether I would ever see her again.

My uncle cared very little for the usual tourist attractions, but suddenly he caught sight of a lofty church tower, which stood on the island of Amak, in the south-west quarter of Copenhagen. We took the steam-ferry which plied along the canals, and soon we were on the island. Through narrow streets we made our way to the church, which was not remarkable except for the fact that there was a spiral staircase winding up round the outside of the steeple.

'Let's climb that steeple,' said my uncle.

'But, Uncle, I've no head for heights; I should be dizzy . . .'

'That is the object of the exercise,' he said firmly. 'To get you used to heights.'

I looked at him in dismay.

'Come along now, don't waste any more time.'

There was no help for it. We called at the caretaker's house and collected the key. My uncle hurried on ahead at a brisk pace, while I followed him. It was all right for the first part of the climb, since we were in an enclosed staircase, but after the first hundred and fifty steps I felt the air blowing into my face – we had come out on to the open platform at the foot of the steeple itself. Then the ordeal began; an airy stairway, protected by a fragile rail, towered above us, the steps grew ever narrower and seemed to reach the sky.

'I can't do it!' I moaned.

'Where's your nerve, boy? There's nothing to it. Come along now!'

He went ahead and I was forced to follow, bending myself double in my terror. The air went to my head, I felt the steeple swaying in the wind, my legs gave way under me, soon I was on hands and knees, then crawling on my belly. I shut my eyes, feeling sick.

At last, with my uncle dragging me by the collar, I came out under the topmost pinnacle.

'Now!' he shouted against the wind, 'look down! You must learn to look down!'

I opened my eyes. Far below I saw the houses, spreading out flat as if they had been crushed by a fall, under the mists of their smoking chimneys. Above my head were floating tatters of cloud; through an optical illusion they appeared motionless while the steeple and myself seemed to be moving at a fantastic speed. In the distance the green country stretched away on one side, while on the other the sea sparkled in the sunlight. The Sound was spread out below, as far as the Point of Elsinore, with a few white sails like seagulls' wings, and in the mist to eastwards the coast of Sweden was faintly outlined. The immense landscape swam before my eyes.

My first lesson in the mastery of height lasted for an hour. When at last I felt the solid pavement under my feet again, I could hardly stand upright.

'We'll have another spell tomorrow,' said my taskmaster.

And so we did, and for four more days after that, till at last, in spite of myself, I did really make definite progress in the art of looking down from a height.

8

Reykjavik

Now at last came our sailing date. A kind friend had given my uncle some letters of introduction to various influential people in Iceland, including the Danish governor, and armed with these, we set off to the quay. Our baggage was taken on board and stowed, and the captain of the *Valkyrie* himself showed us to our little cabins.

'How's the wind?' my uncle asked.

'Fine, fine,' said Captain Bjarne. 'A fresh south-easter, couldn't be better.'

In a very few minutes the schooner with all sails set was ploughing her way through the narrow waters of the Sound. An hour later, the Danish capital was sinking into the distant waves and the *Valkyrie* was off Elsinore. In my nervous excitement I almost expected to see the shade of Hamlet wandering on the legendary cliff.

'Hamlet!' I called softly. 'You, great madman, you would understand our quest! No doubt *you* would be crazy enough to come with us to the centre of the world!' But no ghost answered from the ancient walls, and we sailed on into the Kattegat.

The *Valkyrie* was a good ship, but with a sailing-vessel anything may happen. She was carrying a cargo of coal, household goods, pottery, woollen clothing and wheat; the crew consisted of five men, all Danes.

'How long will the trip take?' my uncle asked the captain.

'About ten days,' he answered, 'that is, if we don't run into any north-westerly squalls round the Faroes.'

'But you usually make the voyage in reasonable time?'

'Don't fret yourself, Professor, we'll get there.'

Indeed, the winds and the waves seemed to be on my uncle's side. The schooner skimmed gracefully forward on her course, so that we made the North Sea crossing in record time, sighted the Scottish coast and then passed between the Orkneys and the Shetlands towards the Faroes. Now the long Atlantic waves were breaking against the little ship, and we had some trouble with adverse winds. My uncle was very seasick, to his great shame and annoyance, and spent the whole time lying down in his cabin. The rough sea had little effect on me, however, and I could not help feeling rather pleased with myself.

About the end of the expected term of ten days, we came through a storm which forced the schooner to run with sails reefed close, and sighted the buoy on Skagaflös, a long headland with dangerous rocks running a great way out under the waves. An Icelandic pilot came aboard, and three hours later we lay at anchor off Reykjavik, in Faxa Bay.

The professor emerged from his cabin at last, not quite up to the mark but still undaunted and with a gleam of satisfaction in his eyes.

The quay was lined with the local population, always

particularly interested in the arrival of a ship, which no doubt brought something for every family.

My uncle was eager to leave his floating prison, or rather hospital. But before we disembarked he led me into the bows and there he pointed out, at the north-western bastion of the vast bay, a high mountain with twin peaks, a double cone shrouded in eternal snow.

'Snaefells!' he cried. 'Snaefells!' Then he laid his finger on his lips in sign of secrecy and climbed down into the waiting boat. I followed, and soon we set foot on Icelandic soil.

A fine-looking man in General's uniform stepped forward: this was Baron Trampe, the governor of the island, in person. My uncle realised who he must be and handed him his letters of introduction. They talked together in Danish for a few moments, while I stood by without understanding a word. The Baron was most affable and put himself entirely at the service of Professor Lidenbrock. We were introduced to various other people of importance, including a charming man who was of the greatest possible help to us. This was Mr Fridriksson, the science master at Reykjavik school. This modest scholar spoke nothing but Icelandic and Latin. He spoke Latin when he came forward to offer us his services, and I was at once at home with him; he was indeed the only person with whom I could hold any conversation during my whole visit.

He was kind enough to put us up in his little house, giving us two of his three rooms, and soon we were installed there. The huge quantity of our luggage astonished the people of Reykjavik.

'Well, Axel,' said my uncle, 'that's the worst part over.'

'How do you mean, the worst part?'

'Now we have nothing to do but to make the descent.'

'Well,' I said dubiously, 'if that's how you look at it; but what about coming up again?'

'We'll cross that bridge when we come to it,' said my uncle casually. 'Now there's no time to waste. I shall visit the library. Perhaps they have some manuscript of Saknussemm's, and it will give me a great deal of pleasure to consult it.'

'Very well, then, I'll take a stroll round the town. Don't you want to do the same?'

'I can't say I'm passionately interested in anything *above* the ground here in Iceland.'

I wandered through the small town, which is built on low-lying, marshy soil between two hills. On one side, a vast bed of lava runs down gently sloping towards the sea. On the other lies Faxa Bay, bounded to the north by the great glacier of Snaefells. At that time the *Valkyrie* was the only vessel in the roads.

In three hours I had visited the town and its neighbourhood as well. It was a mournful landscape; no trees, hardly any vegetation, everywhere the sharp edges of volcanic rocks. The dwellings of the Icelandic peasants are made of earth and turves, with their walls sloping inwards; they look like roofs squatting on the ground. These roofs are in fact the only fertile soil, for they are covered with a growth of luxuriant grass which is carefully scythed and harvested in summer.

Eventually, I returned to Mr Fridriksson's house to find my uncle and his host sitting together.

9

Dinner with Mr Fridriksson

Dinner was ready, my uncle had a ravenous appetite after eating practically nothing during the voyage. The meal was Danish rather than Icelandic, and was not remarkable in itself, but our host, more Icelandic than Danish, was as hospitable as the ancient heroes of the sagas, and piled food on our plates.

The two scholars spoke Icelandic, laced with German by my uncle and with Latin by our host, so that I should not be completely left out. They were discussing scientific questions, but the professor was very careful not to let slip a word about the real reason for his journey to Iceland.

First of all Mr Fridriksson asked after my uncle's visit to the library.

'Your library?' said the professor. 'But I found nothing but a few odd books on almost empty shelves!'

'I should explain,' said our host. 'We believe in letting books be read, not shut up to moulder in bookcases. We have a magnificent library, but the books are all out in the country on long loan, in the homes of our farmers and fishermen. They are all great readers, for during the long dark winter when the sun shows itself for only a few hours a day, they have little to do but read. But now, tell me what you particularly wanted to find in our library?'

My uncle hesitated, then answered: 'I'll tell you, Mr Fridriksson. Among your ancient volumes, have you anything by Arne Saknussemm?'

'Ah, one of our most famous men, but unfortunately we have none of his works. There are none here in Iceland nor anywhere else.'

'But how extraordinary! Why ever not?'

'Because Arne Saknussemm was branded as a heretic, and in 1573 his works were burnt at Copenhagen by the hand of the public executioner.'

'But that's wonderful!' cried the professor. His host was scandalised. 'But of course,' my uncle went on. 'That explains why Saknussemm, under the ban of the Church and forced to hide his brilliant discoveries, was obliged to bury his wonderful secret in a cipher . . .'

'What secret?' said Mr Fridriksson, pricking up his ears.

'A secret . . . well, you know . . .' My uncle tried to cover himself.

'Were you thinking of some particular document?' our host went on.

'No, no, nothing like that . . . I was just imagining . . .'

Mr Fridriksson saw my uncle's embarrassment and was too much of a gentleman to press him. 'I hope,' he went on, tactfully changing the subject, 'that you won't leave our island before making some study of our interesting mineralogy?'

'Certainly,' said my uncle gratefully, 'certainly I hope to discover what I can, if I'm not too late – hasn't your island been thoroughly explored already?'

'By no means,' said Mr Fridriksson, 'there's any amount of work still to be done. Mountains, glaciers, volcanoes – many of them are hardly known. Now to look no further than the view from my window here, that mountain on the horizon, Snaefells . . .'

'Ah, Snaefells!' said my uncle with a deep sigh.

'Now that's a very curious volcano. The crater is worth a visit.'

'It's extinct, then?' said my uncle with an innocent look.

'Yes, it's been extinct for five hundred years.'

'Well, now, that's very interesting,' said my uncle, struggling to keep his excitement under control. 'I think I should like to begin my geological studies with that mountain . . . Saefell – Fessel – what do you call it?'

'Snaefells,' said the kind schoolmaster. They had been speaking in Latin, so that I had been able to follow the conversation. I found it very difficult to keep a straight face, my uncle's expression was so contorted in his efforts to keep his excitement hidden from his host.

'That's a very valuable suggestion of yours,' he went on. 'Yes, I believe we'll attempt to climb Snaefells, we might even have a look at the crater!'

'I wish I could come with you,' said Mr Fridriksson with real regret, 'but unfortunately I have to look after my school. Otherwise I should have been delighted to join you . . .'

'Oh, no!' said my uncle in dismay. 'We don't want to disturb anyone, though it's most kind of you to think of it. Your company would have been of the greatest advantage, but of course, your professional duties . . .'

I hope our host had no notion of my uncle's real feelings.

'You couldn't do better,' said the schoolmaster, 'than to take Snaefells first, but tell me, how will you get there?'

'By sea,' said my uncle. 'It's the most direct route.'

'Yes, of course, but I'm afraid it's out of the question. There isn't a single boat to be had, they're all out fishing on the other side of the island. You'll have to take the route along the coast. It's longer, but much more interesting.'

'Very well, then, I'll have to find a guide. Reliable and intelligent, if possible.'

'I have the very man: he lives at the foot of Snaefells, and earns his living by eider-hunting. A most ingenious man, and he speaks Danish. I'm sure he'll suit you.'

'When can I see him?'

'Tomorrow, if you like.'

'Not today?' My uncle was as impatient as a child.

'He won't be here till tomorrow,' said the schoolmaster smiling.

'Tomorrow, then,' said my uncle with a sigh. However, he was sincerely grateful to his Icelandic host, and we spent a very pleasant evening.

10

Our Guide Hans

I slept soundly in my truckle bed, and in the morning I awoke to hear my uncle chattering away next door. I jumped out of bed and when I was dressed I went into my uncle's room.

He was talking in Danish with a tall, well-built fellow, who looked uncommonly powerful. The man had a large head and a rather simple expression, but his eyes, of a dreamy blue, seemed intelligent. He had long red hair falling over his shoulders; his movements were easy and natural, though he kept his hands and arms still when he spoke; he seemed of a calm and steady nature, by no means lazy, but peaceful. I had the feeling that he asked nothing from anyone, that he worked to suit himself, and that nothing in the world would surprise or upset him.

It was amusing to watch the Icelander as he listened to my uncle's passionate flow of words. He remained unmoved, with folded arms, while my uncle waved his hands wildly; he answered No by a faint shake of the head, and Yes by nodding so slightly that his hair hardly moved on his shoulders.

I could hardly believe that this man was a hunter; he would

be a first-rate stalker, but how could he ever catch his quarry? But later, Mr Fridriksson told me how eiderdown is gathered. The eiderduck makes her nest among the rocks along the fjords and lines it with the fine down she plucks from her breast. Then the hunter comes quietly along and steals the nest, so that the poor bird has to start all over again. At last she has no more down, and her mate is forced to provide the lining for the nest. The drake's down is harsh and coarse, and of little market value, so that the duck is at last allowed to lay her eggs undisturbed. She brings up her brood in peace, but next year the harvest is gathered all over again.

Our guide's name was Hans Bjelke. No one could have been more unlike my uncle, and yet they got on excellently together. Neither of them had any interest in money, so they soon came to terms. Hans agreed to lead us to the village of Stapi, on the south coast of the peninsula, just at the foot of Snaefells. That was twenty-two miles, a two-day journey, according to my uncle. But when he discovered that they were Danish miles of 24,000 feet, he had to think again, and count on about seven or eight days through such rough country.

We hired four horses, one each for my uncle and me, and two for our baggage. Hans would go on foot as he always did. He knew the country like the back of his hand and promised to take us by the shortest route. When we reached Stapi he would continue to serve as our guide during our scientific excursions; his rate of pay was fixed at three rixdollars a week, and the only condition he made was that his wages should be paid to him regularly every Saturday night.

We were to start on 16th June. My uncle wanted to give Hans something on account, but he refused with the word:

'*Efter.*'

'After,' my uncle translated as Hans glided out of the room.

'A fine fellow,' said my uncle. 'Little does he know what's in store for him!'

'Then you're taking him with us . . .'

'Yes, Axel, to the centre of the earth.'

There were forty-eight hours to kill. To my great regret I had to spend them in packing. Everything had to be stowed extremely carefully to stand the rough horseback journey. There were four groups: instruments, firearms, tools and rations.

The instruments were as follows:

1. A centigrade thermometer, registering up to 150 degrees,[1] which seemed to me too much or too little. Too much, if the air-temperature reached that height, for in that case we should be burnt to a cinder. Too little, if we had to measure the temperature of matter in fusion.

2. A special compressed-air barometer, known as a manometer, made to measure pressures greater than that of the atmosphere at sea level. An ordinary barometer would have been useless, since the pressure of the atmosphere was bound to increase proportionately as we went underground.

3. A Swiss chronometer giving the exact time according to the Hamburg meridian.

[1] 302°F.

4. Two special compasses.
5. A telescope.
6. Two electric lamps, worked by Ruhmkorff coils.

For firearms, we had two rifles and two Colt revolvers. Why we took them I had no idea, since we were hardly likely to meet either savage men or wild beasts. My uncle loved them as he loved his instruments, and he was particularly proud of a large quantity of highly explosive gun-cotton, of a particular type unaffected by damp.

Our tools consisted of two picks, two ice-axes, a ladder of silk rope, three steel-tipped sticks, an axe, a hammer, a dozen heavy steel staples and ring-headed bolts, and some long lengths of knotted cord. This made a huge bundle, for the ladder alone was three hundred feet long.

Finally, our rations: they made a small but adequate pack, for I knew that there was a six months' supply of concentrated meat and biscuits. The only liquid we took was gin. There was no water; but we had our flasks, and my uncle was counting on underground springs to fill them. This was a shock to me, for I was sure that the water – if we found any – would be unfit to drink, either boiling hot or tainted by poisonous minerals. But my uncle only scoffed at my old-maidish objections, as he called them.

In addition, we had a medicine chest containing surgical instruments, bandages, disinfectants, etc. – everything necessary for dealing with wounds and broken bones, and even for emergency operations.

My uncle was taking a good stock of tobacco, gunpowder and tinder, and a leather belt buckled round his waist in which he carried a supply of gold, silver and paper currency. There were also six pairs of sturdy boots, waterproofed with rubber and pitch.

'A perfectly equipped expedition!' said my uncle gleefully, looking at the completed packs. 'Nothing can stop us now!'

That evening we went to a grand dinner at the Governor's house. I could not understand a word of the conversation, but I noticed that my uncle talked all the time.

The next day, 15th June, we put the finishing touches to our preparations, and our host was kind enough to present the professor with an excellent map of Iceland, very much better than his old one.

At five o'clock next morning I was wakened by the whinnying of our four horses in the road outside my window. I dressed and went out. Hans was loading up our packs without an unnecessary movement, and without taking the slightest notice of my uncle, who was fussing round making all sorts of suggestions.

By six we were ready to start. Mr Fridriksson was there to see us off; my uncle thanked him in his best Icelandic and I in my best Latin. Then we were in the saddle, trotting off down the road.

11

To Snaefells

It was a cool, cloudy day, the best weather for travelling. As we rode through the unknown countryside my heart was light, and for the first time I began to take some pleasure in the excursion.

'Anyway,' I thought, 'what's the risk? The country is interesting, so I shall enjoy climbing the mountain, and even exploring the crater. I'm sure this fellow Saknussemm did no more than that. We certainly shan't find the way to the centre of the earth.'

Hans walked in the lead at a quick, steady pace. Then came the two pack-horses, then my uncle and I bringing up the rear on our small, sturdy beasts.

Hans led us out of the town and along the coast; we were riding through poor pastures, yellow rather than green. The rocky mountain-tops showed faintly on the misty eastern horizon. Sometimes we caught sight of snowfields gleaming on distant slopes, sometimes we saw sheer summits rising out of the sea of moving cloud like reefs in the sky. Every now and then we came to places where lines of barren rock ran down towards the sea, but there was always room to pass. Our horses instinctively chose the best paths and never slackened speed.

My tall uncle was a most comical sight on his little horse. His feet touched the ground and he looked like a six-legged centaur.

'Good horse, good horse!' he said, patting its neck. 'There is no more intelligent animal than the Icelandic pony, Axel, and nothing stops him – neither snow, nor storm, nor foul ways, nor rocks, nor glaciers. A fine, sober, steady beast! He never puts a hoof wrong. If we come to a river or an arm of the sea – as we certainly shall – it won't make any difference to him, he'll simply plunge straight in and take it in his stride. But it's no good to hurry him. Just let him alone and we'll do our thirty miles a day.'

'That's all right for us,' I said, 'but what about the guide?'

'I'm not worried about him. These people just keep on going; anyway I can always let him have my horse for a spell. I shall get cramp sooner or later. My arms are all right but I have to think of my legs.'

We were making good progress. The country was almost deserted; now and again we saw a lonely farm, built of wood, earth and fragments of lava. There was no road or even path to be seen, and the tracks of rare travellers were soon blotted out by the wind and the creeping grass.

Two hours after leaving Reykjavik we came to Gufunes, a little place of only a few houses. Hans called a halt for half an hour; he shared our frugal meal, answered Yes or No to my uncle's questions, and when he was asked where we were to spend the night, answered simply, 'Garthar.'

46

I looked it up on the map. I found it on the north shore of the Hvalfjord and showed my uncle.

'Splendid!' he said. 'We're getting on.'

Three hours later we came to Kollafjord and made our way round its shores; this was quicker and easier than attempting to cross it. Soon we were at Ejulberg, where the horses were watered. Then we rode on along a narrow strip of land between a range of hills and the sea. In this way we came to Brautarholt, and then to Saurbaer on the southern shore of Hvalfjord.

It was four o'clock in the afternoon. We looked across the broad waters of the fjord. The waves were thundering on the jagged rocks, while the gulf churned out between rock-walls a thousand feet high. However intelligent our horses were, I did not relish the idea of crossing that arm of the sea on horseback.

'If they're as intelligent as all that,' I thought, 'they certainly won't attempt it. And I'm far too intelligent to let them try.'

But my uncle did not hesitate; he rode his horse right down to the water's edge. The creature sniffed and drew back; the rider urged it forward. The horse refused, with a toss of its head. Then my uncle started swearing and beating the pony, which reared up, snorting, and tried to throw him. At last the little horse crouched low and slid out from under its rider, leaving him standing at the very edge of the sea.

'Damn the brute!' he said, feeling rather ridiculous.

'*Farja*,' said the guide, tapping him on the shoulder.

'What? A ferry?'

'*Der*,' said Hans, pointing to a boat.

'Well, why ever didn't you say so before?' cried my uncle. 'What are we waiting for, then?'

'*Tidvatten*,' said the guide.

'Oh, we have to wait for the tide. What a bore.'

I realised why. The ebbing or flowing of the water would cause such a strong current in the mouth of the fjord that we should either be dragged out to sea or swept up to the head of the gulf, unless we waited for the turn of the tide.

At last, at six o'clock, the moment came. Our party, with the two ferrymen and the four horses, went aboard a rather frail, flat-bottomed boat. I was accustomed to the Elbe steam-ferries and thought the rowers' oars a feeble source of power. It took us more than an hour to cross the fjord, but at last we were all over safely. Half an hour later we reached Garthar.

12

Icelandic Hospitality

It should have been dark, but in those polar regions it is never completely dark at night in summer, and during June and July the sun does not set at all. But the temperature had fallen, and I was cold and very hungry. I was glad indeed to reach the farmstead where we were to put up.

It was a peasant's house, but no first-class hotel would have given us so warm a welcome. When we came to the door, the master of the house came out to take us by the hand, and without further ado he led us in. He took us to the guest-room, a large room with a floor of beaten earth and a window covered with the membrane of a sheep, not very transparent. For beds there were two box-like wooden frames, painted red and decorated with Icelandic proverbs, and filled with dry hay. I had not been expecting so much comfort; on the other hand, the whole house reeked with the strong smell of dried fish, pickled meat and sour milk.

When we had taken off our outer clothing, we were called into the kitchen, where a fire was burning. It was a primitive hearth – a stone in the middle of the room, and a hole in the roof to let out the smoke.

As we came in, the host saluted us with the word '*saellvertu*', which means 'be happy', and kissed us on the cheek. Then his wife repeated the same greeting and kissed us in her turn, after which they both laid their right hands on their hearts and bowed low. I should tell you that the farmer's wife was the mother of nineteen children; they were all there, big and little, swarming about among the wreaths of smoke that filled the room. Every now and again a little blond head with a rather melancholy expression would pop up out of the smoke. They looked like a band of grubby cherubs.

My uncle and I were delighted with these urchins, and soon we had three or four of them on our backs, as many on our knees and the rest crawling round our feet. Those who could speak repeated '*saellvertu*' in every possible tone of voice. Even the babies welcomed us with squeals of joy.

Just as the meal was ready, Hans came in. He had been seeing to the horses; that is, he had turned them loose to seek their pasture among the scanty sea-grass and rock-lichen. Next morning they would show up again, ready for work.

'*Saellvertu*,' said Hans at the door. Then very calmly and almost mechanically, he kissed the host, the hostess, and all nineteen children in turn, making no difference between them.

When this ceremony was over, we sat down twenty-four to table, which meant that some were literally on top of others; the luckiest had only two children on their knees!

As soon as the soup was served, the talking stopped. We had lichen soup, not bad at all, then a huge slab of dried fish swimming in a sea of sour butter, which the Icelanders prefer to fresh butter. Then came *skyr*, a sort of sour curd, flavoured with the juice of juniper berries and eaten with biscuits; and to drink, a kind of buttermilk called *blanda*. I have no idea whether this strange meal could be called good or not, but I was hungry and ate ravenously, down to the last spoonful of the thick buckwheat porridge which was served for dessert.

After the meal the children slipped quietly away, while the grown-ups sat round the smouldering mass of peat, heather-roots, cow-dung and dried fish-bones which served as a fire. After we had warmed ourselves we retired to our rooms. The hostess, according to custom, offered to pull off our stockings and trousers for us; we refused as gracefully as we could, and she did not insist. At last I was slumbering peacefully on my bed of hay.

Next morning at five o'clock, when we said goodbye to the Icelandic peasant, my uncle had a great deal of difficulty in getting him to accept suitable payment.

A hundred yards from Garthar the ground began to change. It became marshy and the going was rather sticky. To our right, the mountain range stretched away like a vast system of natural fortifications. Often there were streams which we had to ford, keeping the baggage as dry as possible.

Now we were in the barren desert, and the last blades of grass had vanished from our path. No trees, except for a few dwarf birches like reptiles clawing sideways along the ground. No animals but a few half-starved horses straying in the desolate plains. Sometimes a hawk hovered in the grey clouds, then veered away southwards with beating wings. I was overcome by the melancholy of this wild land and was sick for the gentle countryside of home.

That evening we forded two rivers rich in trout and pike, the Alfa and the Heta. We had to spend the night in a deserted hovel, which felt as if it were haunted by the trolls in which the country people still firmly believe. The frost demon certainly had his dwelling there, and held us through the night in his icy clutch.

Another day's journey through the same desolate country brought us to Krosolbt, and half the distance was behind us.

On 19th June we crossed a long stretch of lava desert, called *hraun* in Icelandic. The wrinkled surface of the rock spread out in strange formations, like ropes lying along the ground or coiled up. This huge, petrified sea had originally flowed as molten lava from the summits of the neighbouring mountains, cold and extinct now, but once in violent activity. Only a few puffs of steam from hot springs rose here and there from cracks in the ground.

It was a curious landscape, and we would have liked to linger and study it, but we had to get on. Soon the soil became marshy again, with little lakes. Now we were heading west, after rounding the great bay of Faxa, and the white summit of Snaefells with its twin cones shone out through the clouds less than twenty miles away.

The horses went splendidly, taking the difficult ground in their stride. I must confess that I was beginning to feel exhausted, but my uncle was as spry and hearty as on the first day. I was full of admiration for him; he seemed to be doing as well as the guide, to whom the whole expedition was no more than a country walk.

On Saturday, 20th June, at six o'clock in the evening, we reached Büdir, a village on the coast, and the guide received his first pay-packet. We put up that night with Hans's own family, that is to say, his uncles and cousins. They were very kind, and I should have liked to stay with them for a few days to recuperate. But the idea of taking a rest never occurred to my uncle, and the next day as usual we were in the saddle again.

Now we were skirting the huge base of the volcano. Like a mighty oak, it sent its granite roots through the nearby country, where now and again they stuck out above the ground. The professor could not keep his eyes off the mountain, he waved his arms towards it as if he were a knight-errant challenging a giant. At last, after a long day's journey, the horses stopped of their own accord at the door of the parsonage at Stapi.

13

My Last Vain Plea

Stapi is a village of about thirty cabins, built on the lava rock at the foot of the volcano. It lies at the head of a little fjord enclosed by a wall of basalt.

Everyone knows that basalt is a black or dark brown rock formed by the action of fire, it takes geometrical forms as if nature in creating it had worked with set-square, compass and plumb-line. Of course I had heard of the Giant's Causeway in Ireland, and of Fingal's Cave in the Hebrides, but I had never seen any basaltic structure for myself, and Stapi is a fine example.

The wall of the fjord, and indeed the whole coast of the peninsula, was formed of huge upright columns, thirty feet high. These straight shafts, of pure geometrical form, supported others which had fallen across them like triumphal arches. Every now and then there were natural gateways through which the sea thundered, breaking in foam. Fragments of basalt pillars, torn down by the fury of the waves, lay along the ground like the ruins of an ancient temple of the northern gods.

This was a fitting end to our overland journey. Hans had

guided us skilfully, and it was a comfort to think that he would still be with us for the next, most terrifying part of the expedition.

As we came to the door of the parsonage – a low cabin just like the rest – I saw a man in leather apron, his hammer in his hand, shoeing a horse.

'*Saellvertu*,' said the hunter.

'*God dag*,' replied the blacksmith in Danish.

'*Kyrkoherde*,' said Hans.

'The pastor!' said my uncle. 'Axel, it seems that this good man is the pastor.'

Meanwhile the guide was explaining the situation to the minister. He threw down his hammer and gave a sort of whinny, and a tall fierce woman like a troll-wife strode out of the hut. I was terrified she would kiss us, but there was nothing of that, and she led us indoors with a sulky face.

The guest-room was small, filthy, and evil-smelling, but we had no choice. The pastor was a jack-of-all-trades; as well as blacksmith he was fisherman, hunter, and carpenter. But perhaps he made up for it on Sundays. It was not his fault; these poor country clergymen are miserably paid and have to make their living as well as they can. My uncle decided not to linger here but to gain the cleaner air of the mountain at the earliest possible moment. He therefore made all haste with the arrangements for our climb. Hans hired three Icelandic porters to take the place of the horses; they were to carry our equipment up the mountain and into the bowl of the crater, and then they would leave us to shift for ourselves.

At this stage, my uncle was at last obliged to tell the eider-hunter the real object of his expedition. Hans never turned a hair. It was all one to him whether he stayed above his island soil or plunged into its bowels. I admired his calm, but for myself, now that we were almost literally on the brink, all my fears returned. Was it too late to draw back? I was bitterly aware that I should have made my stand against my headstrong uncle at Hamburg and not at the foot of Snaefells.

There was one particular thought which came to me then, and drove me almost out of my mind with terror. I tried to face the situation as calmly as I could.

'Now,' I said to myself, 'we're going to climb Snaefells. All right. We're going to visit the crater. So far so good, others have done the same and lived to tell the tale. But that's not the end of it. If we really find a passage leading downwards, if the wretched Saknussemm wasn't inventing it, then we shall be lost in the subterranean galleries of a volcano. But how do we know that Snaefells is really extinct? How can we tell that a new eruption won't break out at any moment? Because the monster has been sleeping since 1219, does it follow that it can't wake up? And if it does!'

Once this thought had crept into my mind, there was no getting rid of it. At last I decided to speak to my uncle. Surely he might be brought to see reason! I went to find him and told him of my fears, keeping well back in case he turned on me in rage.

'Yes, I've been thinking of that,' he answered calmly.

I had a moment's hope that he would give up the whole crazy plan. I waited, holding my breath.

'I've been thinking about it ever since we arrived at Stapi,' he went on, 'for we must not take unnecessary risks.'

'*No!*' I agreed. 'Certainly not!'

'Snaefells has been silent for six hundred years, but it may yet speak. Now it is always possible to tell in advance whether an eruption is going to take place; I have therefore talked with the villagers and studied the ground, and I can tell you quite definitely, Axel, there will be no eruption.' When I said nothing, he went on: 'You don't believe me? All right, come with me.'

I followed him in despair. He led the way along a passage through the rock wall, away from the sea. Soon we were in flat country, if that name can be given to a vast scrap-heap of volcanic debris; the land seemed to have been crushed by a hail of rocks – basalt, granite and obsidian. Here and there were fumaroles – jets of white steam called '*reykir*' in Icelandic, which came from hot springs and by their energy showed the volcanic activity underground. They seemed to justify my fears. So I nearly fell over backwards with astonishment when the professor said:

'You see these jets of steam, Axel? Well, they prove that we have nothing to fear from the volcano.'

I was speechless.

'Listen,' he went on. 'When there's going to be an eruption, all these steam-holes are tremendously active for a time, then during the actual eruption, they disappear entirely – this is because they are drawn into the main stream of the exploding matter rushing up through the crater. But I am assured that there is nothing unusual about them at present, this is their normal state. Another thing, before an eruption there is a peculiar kind of still, heavy atmosphere, nothing like this ordinary windy weather with a little rain. So you may be quite sure we're safe from that particular trouble.'

I went back to the parsonage with a heavy heart. My uncle had flattened me with his scientific arguments, and I could see only one gleam of hope – that we should find no underground opening, and then we would be simply unable to continue, in spite of all the Saknussemms in the world.

I spent another night of terror – it might be my last in this world! As I tossed about restlessly in my uncomfortable bed, I imagined myself shooting out of the crater's mouth like a rocket into interplanetary space.

The next day, 23rd June, Hans was waiting for us with the porters loaded up with our rations, tools and instruments. Two steel-tipped sticks, two rifles, and two cartridge-belts were reserved for my uncle and me, Hans had taken the precaution of bringing a goatskin full of water, which together with our flasks, would keep us supplied for eight days.

It was nine in the morning. The pastor and his wife stood outside their door to see us off, their farewell taking the form of a perfectly outrageous bill. My uncle paid up without a word. A man setting off for the centre of the world does not haggle over a few paltry rixdollars.

14

Snaefells

Snaefells is five thousand feet high. From our starting-point we could not see the double cone of the summit, only an enormous ice-cap drawn down over the giant's forehead.

We were in single file, with Hans in the lead; he led us by narrow paths not wide enough for two abreast. First we crossed a vast peat-bed, where there was enough fuel to warm the entire population of Iceland for a hundred years. Then the way became more and more difficult. The ground was rising; every now and again we dislodged loose stones which set off falls of rock. These could be dangerous for those behind us so that we had to take great care where we set our feet.

Hans went as calmly as if on a level road; sometimes he disappeared behind a great block and was lost to our sight, then a shrill whistle from his lips would tell us which way he had gone. Often he stopped and set up little heaps of stones by way of a trail to guide us on our return. It was a good idea, but in the event it was useless to us, though no doubt it helped the porters.

After three hours of wearisome scrambling we were only at

the foot of the mountain. There Hans called a halt, and we ate our lunch. My uncle gobbled up his rations, eager to be on the road again, but the guide had more sense; he made us rest for an hour before he gave the signal to go on. The three porters, as niggard of speech as their friend the eider-hunter, did not speak a word and ate sparingly.

Then we began the climb proper. The snowy summit of Snaefells, through an optical illusion common among mountains, appeared very close, and yet, what long hours of back-breaking effort before we should reach it! The stones, with no cement of earth or grass to bind them, rolled away under our feet and went bouncing down into the plain, gathering speed as they fell.

In certain places there were screes as steep as the roof of a house; it was impossible to climb them and we had to make our way round. In these places we helped each other by means of our sticks.

I should tell you that my uncle kept as close to me as he could all the time; he never let me out of his sight and many times he gave me a hand when I needed it. He must have been a born climber himself, for he never lost his balance. The Icelanders, loaded as they were, climbed like mountain goats.

When I looked up at the summit of the mountain towering above us, it seemed impossible to me that we could climb it from this side, unless the slopes became less steep. But luckily for us, after a gruelling hour, in the midst of the vast blanket of snow lying on the shoulder of the volcano we came unexpectedly to a sort of stairway which helped us a great deal. This flight of steps had been formed by one of those torrents of rocks thrown out by eruptions, called ‘*steinar*’ in Icelandic. If this torrent had not been held up by the shape of the mountain, it would have rushed down into the sea and made new islands.

But there it was and it served us well; the steepness of the slope increased, but these stone steps made it possible to climb easily, and indeed almost quickly. I found this out when I stopped for a moment while the others went on; when I looked after them they had already dwindled in the distance to the size of mice.

By seven in the evening we had climbed the two thousand steps of the staircase and were standing on a sort of platform from which rose the cone of the crater itself. It was violently cold, and a fierce wind was blowing. I was exhausted. The professor noticed my plight and decided to call a halt, in spite of his impatience. So he made a sign to the guide, but Hans only shook his head saying, '*Ofvanför.*'

'He means we must go higher,' my uncle explained, then he asked why.

'*Mistour*,' answered the guide.

'*Ja, mistour*,' said one of the others in a tone of alarm.

'What are they saying?' I asked anxiously.

'Look there!' cried my uncle.

I looked out over the plain and saw an immense pillar of powdered pumice, sand and dust rising and twisting like a waterspout; the wind was blowing it towards the side of Snaefells where we stood; it hung like a thick curtain against the sun and cast a huge shadow on the mountain. If this pillar of sand were to lean over, we should certainly be caught up in its eddying whirl. The Icelanders know this kind of vertical dust-storm only too well, when the wind blows from the glaciers, and call it '*mistour*'.

'*Hastigt, hastigt,*' cried Hans, and we all rushed helter-skelter round the side of the mountain, to get out of the path of the oncoming storm. Soon it hurtled against the mountain-side, the earth trembled, there was a hail of stones as in an eruption. By then we were safe behind a sheltering slope; if we had stayed where we were, our bodies would have been mangled and ground to dust, and scattered far and wide like ashes from an unknown meteorite.

Even so, Hans did not think it wise to spend the night on the outside of the cone. We went on climbing on a zigzag course, so that the fifteen hundred feet we still had to climb took almost five hours. The rarefied air made breathing difficult; I was almost at my last gasp, fainting with cold and hunger.

Finally, at eleven at night, in almost total darkness, we reached the summit of Snaefells. Before I sank gratefully down into the shelter of the crater, I caught a glimpse of the midnight sun, at its lowest point, throwing faint gleams over the island sleeping at our feet.

15

Into the Crater

We made short work of our supper, then settled down for the night as best we could. We had hard beds and poor shelter in that awkward camping-ground, five thousand feet above sea level. And yet I sank almost at once into a deep and peaceful sleep; it was the best night I had had for a very long time. I did not even dream.

The next morning I awoke half-frozen in the bitter air. But the sun was shining brightly, and I got up from my granite bed and went to enjoy the view. We were on top of one of the twin peaks of Snaefells – the southern peak. I found I could see over most of the island; from that height the horizon appeared raised, while the centre sank down low into itself. The country lay below me like a relief map; I saw deep valleys running into each other on every side, precipices diminished to the size of wells, lakes looking like ponds, rivers like brooks. On my right, glaciers and mountains ran away into the distance, some of the peaks crested with light plumes of smoke. The mountain range with its snowfields looked like a foaming sea. When I turned towards the west, there was the sea itself in all its vast expanse, like a continuation of the fleecy range; it was difficult to make out the line where the land ended and the sea began. I lost myself in delight, that special excitement of high places which all mountaineers know, and this time I was not dizzy, for I had grown used to heights. Up there in the morning sunshine, on the dazzling snowfield, I felt as light and transparent as the air and the sunlight itself.

But I was brought down to earth again by the professor and Hans, who came to stand beside me on the peak. My uncle gazed over the sea to the west, then he pointed out a light mist or vapour on the distant horizon.

'Greenland,' he said. I was amazed. 'Yes, Greenland,' he went on, 'and when the ice breaks up in the spring, sometimes polar bears come as far as Iceland, drifting on floes. But now to business. Here we are on the top of Snaefells. We have two peaks, the south and the north. Hans will tell us the name given by the Icelanders to the peak we are standing on at present.'

He turned to Hans and spoke in Danish.

'Scartaris,' said the guide.

My uncle looked at me in triumph. 'To the crater!' he said.

The crater was about a mile and a half across and two thousand feet deep. I wondered how it would look if it were filled with flames and thunder. The bottom of the funnel looked no more than about a hundred and fifty yards round, and the slopes leading downwards were not very steep. I could not help thinking of the wide-mouthed barrel of a blunderbuss, and this was not a comforting idea.

'To go down the barrel of a blunderbuss,' I thought, 'when it's very likely loaded and will go off at the least touch; it's crazy!'

But there was no help for it. Hans, unmoved as ever, took the lead, and I joined the party without a word.

Hans did not attempt to climb straight down, he made long zigzags. We were scrambling among loose rocks, and every now and again a rock would overbalance and go bouncing down into the abyss, setting up booming echoes with every bound. Sometimes we had to cross glaciers; Hans took them with the utmost care, probing for crevasses with his steel-tipped stick. Once or twice he thought it necessary for us to be roped together; he was on unknown territory and did not want to take risks. In the end we arrived safe and sound, except for a coil of rope dropped by one of the porters, which shot down ahead of us into the depths. At midday we stood at the bottom of the crater. I looked up and saw an almost round patch of sky, which seemed to have shrunk alarmingly. On one side I saw the peak of Scartaris towering into the sky.

At the bottom of the crater were three chimneys, holes through which the molten lava had belched upwards during the eruptions of Snaefells. Each of these chimneys was about thirty yards across. They gaped beneath our feet; I shrank from looking closer. Professor Lidenbrock ran from one to the other, breathless, waving and shouting words I could not catch. Hans and his mates sat on blocks of lava, watching him, no doubt thinking he was demented.

Suddenly my uncle gave a cry; I thought he must have lost his balance and gone head first down one of the holes. But no, he was standing stock still, his arms flung wide, his legs apart, like stout Cortez on his peak. He was riveted to the ground in front of a granite rock in the centre of the crater.

'Axel!' he shouted. 'Come here!' I ran to join him, leaving the Icelanders standing where they were.

I shared his amazement if not his joy when I read on the western face of the stone block, in runic characters half eaten away by time, that accursed name:

'Arne Saknussemm!' my uncle cried. *'Now* do you believe?'

I could not speak. I went back to my lava seat, overwhelmed by the weight of evidence. At last I raised my head from my despairing thoughts and saw only my uncle and Hans with me in the crater. The porters had been paid off, and were now climbing down the mountain-side on their way back to Stapi.

Hans was sleeping peacefully at the foot of a rock, where he had scooped himself out a bed among the lava. My uncle was pacing about in the bottom of the crater like a wild beast in a trapper's pit. I had neither the will nor the strength to rouse myself, and following the guide's example, I lay down and fell into a disturbed sleep, believing all the time that I could hear rumblings and feel the earth trembling beneath me. So passed the first night in the crater.

The next day the sky above the mountain was grey and overcast. It was my uncle's rage rather than the darkness of the gulf where we lay which first made me aware of this. I realised at once why he was so angry, and the thought gave me a gleam of hope. We had to find out which of the three chimneys was Saknussemm's route, and this would be made plain to us when the shadow of Scartaris touched the right chimney during the last days of June. The peak was indeed the finger of an immense sundial and its shadow on a given day would point our road to the centre of the earth.

But no sun, no shadow. It was 25th June. If the sky would only remain clouded for six days, then we should be forced to put off our observation for another year.

I refrain from describing the helpless fury of Professor Lidenbrock. The day wore on, but the cloud never lifted. Hans did not move from his place; he must have wondered what we were waiting for, if he ever wondered about anything. My uncle did not speak a word to me. He stared continually into the sky, trying to pierce its grey and gloomy heights.

On the 26th there was still no sun, and sleet fell all day. Hans built a hut with blocks of lava. I found what amusement I could in watching the thousands of little waterfalls tumbling down the sloping sides of the crater, and in listening to their noise mingled with that of the stones and gravel.

My uncle was beside himself; and it was certainly enough to try the patience of a saint. But in the end his obstinacy, if not his patience, was rewarded.

Next day there was still no sun, but on Sunday, 28th June, with the new moon came a change in the weather. The sun streamed into the crater. Every little hillock, every rock, every stone was bathed in sunlight and shot its shadow along the ground. Among all these shadows, that of Scartaris stood out like a long, sharp tongue, moving round with the sun.

My uncle moved round with it.

At noon, when the shadow was at its shortest, its point

touched the lip of the central chimney. The professor gave a cry of joy. Then he spoke, in Danish:

'To the centre of the earth!' I looked at Hans.

'*Forüt*,' he said calmly.

'Let's go,' said my uncle, trembling with excitement.

16

Down the Chimney

This was the real thing. Till this minute, our journey had been tiring rather than difficult; the test faced us now.

I had not yet dared to look down that terrible hole. It was the moment of final decision: I could go forward or I could refuse. But I found I could not run away in front of Hans. He accepted the adventure so quietly, he seemed to be so perfectly indifferent to the danger, that I was shamed into pretending to be as fearless as he was. If I had been alone with my uncle, I would have started arguing again, but as it was I said nothing. I remembered Gretel and her brave words, and went up to the central chimney.

As I said before, it was about thirty yards across, or ninety yards round. I stood on an overhanging rock and leaned forward, looking down. I felt my hair rising on my scalp; I was drawn irresistibly towards the yawning hole. I was tottering, my head felt light, I was beginning to lose my balance . . . A hand gripped my arm, the guide's hand. It seemed as if I had forgotten all my lessons on the church tower in Copenhagen.

My terrified glance down the chimney had been enough to give me an idea of the problem. The walls were almost sheer, though there were plenty of foot-holds. The jutting rocks made a sort of staircase with no handrail. We needed a rope, but how could we untie it when we had climbed down its length?

My uncle found a very simple means to get round this difficulty. He unrolled a coil of rope about as thick as a thumb and four hundred feet long; he let half of it down the chimney, then passed the other half round a block of lava before dropping it down beside the first half. So there was the rope looped round the block, and all we had to do was to climb down one by one, grasping the two ropes. When we had all three reached the two-hundred-foot limit, we had only to let go of one end and pull on the other till the whole rope had come down beside us. And so on, for ever.

'Now for the baggage,' said my uncle as he finished arranging the rope. 'It must be split up into three packs, one for each of us – I mean only the fragile objects. Hans, you take the tools and a third of the food; you, Axel, the guns and the second third of the food; and I will take the rest of the food and the delicate instruments.'

'Who's going to take all these ropes and ladders, and the clothing?' I asked.

'No trouble about *them*,' the professor answered. 'They'll take themselves.'

My uncle's ideas had the simplicity of genius. He told Hans to make a huge bundle of all the unbreakable baggage, which was then securely corded and pushed over the edge. It rumbled thundering into the abyss, echoing round the walls as it fell.

My uncle leaned over the edge and watched it out of sight, then stood upright with a satisfied smile.

'Good,' he said, 'now for us.'

This was it! I shuddered.

We strapped on our packs and made ready to go: Hans, then my uncle, then myself. There was silence as we scrambled down, except for the sound of rocks falling into the depths.

When my turn came, I let myself slide, frantically holding the double rope with one hand, and steadying myself with my stick in the other. I had one desperate fear: that the rock would give way. And the rope seemed to me very slender to bear the weight of three men. I used it as little as I could help, balancing like a trapeze artist on pieces of lava, grasping them with my feet like a monkey.

When Hans by misfortune kicked a rock loose, he called in his calm voice:

'*Gif akt!*'

'Look out!' my uncle cried.

Half an hour later we were all on top of a rock deeply embedded in the wall of the chimney. Hans pulled one end of the rope, the other flew up, and soon the whole rope was tumbling down on top of us, together with a shower of sharp stones.

I leaned cautiously over the edge of our platform and could see no bottom to the hole.

We repeated the operation, and half an hour later we were a further two hundred feet down. Any geologist slithering down into the bowels of the earth like this would surely have been out of his mind if he had tried to study the rocks he passed in his headlong descent. As for me, it was all one to me whether

71

they were Pliocene, Miocene, Eocene, Cretaceous, Jurassic, Triassic, Permian, Carboniferous, Devonian, Silurian or primitive. I only knew they were all very hard and hurt me as I banged against them. But my uncle the professor had evidently taken notes, because on one of our halts he said to me:

'The farther I go the more confident I become: the primordial nature of the rock leads me to believe that there is no central furnace. Anyway, we'll soon see.'

I was not in the mood to argue. My silence was taken for agreement, and we went on with our descent.

After three hours I could still see no bottom to the chimney. When I looked up I could see a tiny circle of sky; it was growing dark. But as we climbed still deeper it seemed to me that the echoes set up by the falling stones had a dull ring, as if the bottom were not so very distant now. As I had taken careful note of our operations with the rope, I could tell almost exactly how deep we were and how much time had passed. We had made the manoeuvre fourteen times, and each time took half an hour. That was seven hours, plus fourteen fifteen-minute rests, or three and a half hours. Ten and a half hours altogether. We had started shortly after one o'clock, then it must be about eleven now.

As for the depth, these fourteen descents of two hundred feet made two thousand eight hundred feet. As I reached this conclusion I heard Hans calling:

'Halt!'

I stopped short, almost kicking my uncle on the head.

'Here we are!' he said.

'Where?' I asked, sliding down beside him.

72

'At the bottom of the perpendicular chimney.'

'Is there a way out?'

'Yes, I think so, there seems to be a sort of passage slanting away towards the right. We'll see tomorrow. We'll eat now and then sleep.'

It was not entirely dark. We opened one of the food packs, ate our supper, and lay down on the tumbled rocks. As I lay on my back and looked upwards I saw a brilliant speck at the end of this three-thousand-foot tube. It was a star, belonging, I thought, to the Little Bear. I fell into a deep sleep.

17

In the Bowels of the Earth

At eight o'clock in the morning, a ray of daylight came to wake us. It shone on the lava walls and was broken up into a rain of sparks by the facets of the rock. It was strong enough to show us our surroundings.

'Well, Axel, what do you think of this?' said my uncle, sitting up and rubbing his hands. 'Have you ever slept so peacefully in our house at home? No rumble of carts, no cries of street-sellers, no boatmen's shouts!'

'Oh, it's quiet enough, at the bottom of this well, but it's a frightening sort of quiet.'

'Now really, Axel,' said my uncle, 'if you're frightened already, what will it be like later on? We haven't gone an inch down into the earth yet.'

'What do you mean?'

'Only that we're at the level of the island itself! This long tube leading down from the crater of Snaefells ends roughly at sea level.'

'How do you know?'

'Look at the barometer.' I looked, and saw that it showed

only the ordinary pressure of the air at sea level. 'Soon we'll have to use the manometer,' said my uncle.

'But won't the increased pressure be very painful to us?' I asked.

'I don't think so. We shall go down slowly, and our lungs will grow used to breathing a denser atmosphere. High-altitude fliers grow short of air; perhaps we shall have too much, but it's better that way. Now, let's not waste time. Where's that bundle we dropped down ahead of us?'

I remembered that we had looked for it the night before, but without success. My uncle spoke to Hans, who looked all round with his hunter's eyes, then cried:

'*Der huppe!*'

'Up there − yes, so it is.' It had lodged on a ledge of rock about a hundred feet above our heads. The Icelander clambered up like a cat and soon the bundle bounced down beside us.

'Now,' said my uncle, 'let's have breakfast, and we'll make it a celebration, before starting on our long trek.'

Accordingly our biscuit and dried meat were washed down, on this occasion, with gin and water. After breakfast, my uncle took out the notebook in which he intended to keep a log of our journey; he took his various instruments and jotted down the following data:

Sunday, 28th June
Chronometer: 8.17 a.m.
Barometer: 29·7
Thermometer: 6°[1]
Direction: E.S.E.

[1]42°F.

75

This last observation, taken by means of the compass, referred to the dark passage.

'Now, Axel,' said the professor, cheerful and excited, 'we're really going down into the bowels of the earth. This is the precise moment our journey begins!' Grasping his Ruhmkorff coil in one hand, he switched on the current with the other, and a fairly bright beam of light shone down the gallery. Hans carried the other lamp. These electric lights were of the greatest value to us, being perfectly safe even among the most inflammable gases.

We took up our packs and set off. Hans pushed the big bundle in front of him, and I brought up the rear. Just before stepping into the dark passage I looked up, and at the end of the long tube I saw the sky of Iceland, which I was never to set eyes on again.

The tunnel we were now entering had served as a path for the lava during the eruption of 1219. It had coated the interior with a thick, brilliant glaze, which reflected our electric lamps in multiple dazzling images. Our chief difficulty was not to slide too fast down the slope of almost forty-five degrees; luckily there were hollow places as well as heat-blisters which served as steps, and we went cautiously down, our luggage running ahead of us at the end of a long rope.

The glassy rock which formed steps under our feet had formed stalactites on the roof and walls of the tunnel; the lava, porous in some places, swelled into little round bulbs; crystals of opaque quartz, jewelled with drops of clear glass and hanging from the vault like candelabra, lit up as our lights picked them out. I remembered the fairy-tales of my childhood, the genii with their underground palaces, blazing with lights to receive the mortal prince.

'This is terrific!' I cried. 'Look at the colours, Uncle – the way the lava changes from red to brown, then to brilliant yellow – those hanging crystals like balls of fire!'

'My dear Axel, this from you!' My uncle was delighted at my first signs of enthusiasm. 'But you haven't seen anything yet! Onward! Let's go on!'

He might just as well have said, 'Let's slide on,' because we were sliding tirelessly down the long sloping corridor of the underworld; I thought of Virgil's *facilis descensus Averni*, the easy path to Hell. I often looked at the compass; it was always set to the south-east. The lava flow ran on as straight as a Roman road.

Meanwhile, the temperature did not rise very much. I was astonished whenever I looked at the thermometer. Two hours after the start, it was only 10 degrees,[1] or 4 degrees[2] higher than at the beginning. This made me think that our route was horizontal rather than vertical. It was easy to know exactly how deep we were. The professor was taking careful measurements of the angles as we went, but he kept his findings to himself.

At about eight o'clock in the evening he decided to call it a day. Hans sat down and the lamps were hung on projecting rocks. We were in a sort of cave where there was plenty of air – indeed, it was very draughty. I wondered where these draughts came from, but not very seriously, because I was too hungry and too tired. The seven hours' descent had exhausted me, and I was delighted when I heard the halt called. Hans spread out some provisions on a block of lava, and we ate. But

[1] 50°F.
[2] 39°F.

77

I was worried about one thing: our water supply was half consumed. My uncle had been counting on underground springs, but up to now there had been no sign of water. I asked him what he thought.

'You're surprised that we've found no water yet?'

'Yes, and I'm rather anxious; we haven't enough to last us for more than five days.'

'Don't worry, Axel, we'll certainly find water, probably more than we want.'

'When?'

'When we've got through this crust of lava. How do you think that springs could break through these walls?'

'But perhaps the lava goes down very deep?' I asked. 'It seems to me that we haven't yet made much progress downwards?'

'Why do you think that?'

'Because it ought to be very much hotter,' I said.

'That's your theory,' said my uncle. 'What does the thermometer say?'

'Fifteen degrees,[1] which is only about nine degrees hotter than when we started.'

'All right, so what's your explanation?'

'I'll tell you,' I said. 'According to most authorities, the temperature in the earth increases one degree for every one hundred feet. But there are various conditions which may modify this scale. Near an extinct volcano, for example, when there is an insulating layer of gneiss, it has been noticed that the temperature rises one degree only every one hundred and

[1] 59°F

twenty-five feet. If you multiply nine by one hundred and twenty-five you get one thousand one hundred and twenty-five feet. I calculate, therefore, that we are only one thousand one hundred and twenty-five feet below sea level.'

'Your arithmetic is perfectly correct, only unfortunately it doesn't tie up with my observations from measuring the angles.'

'What do you think, then, Uncle?'

'I think that we are now ten thousand feet below sea level.'

The professor's calculations were correct, and we were already six thousand feet deeper than the greatest recorded depths ever reached by man, such as the mines at Kitzbühel in the Tyrol, and some others in Bohemia. But the temperature, which should have been eighty-one degrees[1] at this depth, was scarcely fifteen. It was very strange.

[1] 178°F

18

The Wrong Turning

The next day, Tuesday, 30th June, at six o'clock, we went on with our journey.

We were still following the gentle natural slope of the lava tunnel. At 12.17 p.m. exactly we came to the end of the corridor, and found ourselves with a problem. We were at a crossroads, facing a choice of two dark, narrow passages. Which ought we to take?

My uncle, not wanting to hesitate in front of the guide or of me, chose the eastern tunnel, and we went on. In any case, there was absolutely nothing to choose between them; we might just as well have tossed a coin.

The new gallery hardly sloped at all. It was very uneven in height and width; sometimes we were under high pointed arches like the aisles of a Gothic cathedral; at other times we had to stoop to pass under low vaults propped up by squat pillars. Then again, we came to places like the tunnels of moles, where we had to crawl.

The temperature never became unbearably hot. I could not help thinking how it would have been when these peaceful ways were the channels for molten lava, when flaming torrents surged round the corners of the gallery, mixed with explosive gases!

'Let's hope the old volcano doesn't get any fancy ideas,' I was thinking. But I said nothing of my worries to my uncle Otto, who simply would not have understood them. He went straight ahead, walking, sliding, even tumbling, with a firmness of purpose which I could only admire.

At six in the evening, after an easy day, we had made six miles to the south but hardly a quarter of a mile in depth. My uncle called a halt, and we ate our supper and lay down to sleep, with very little fuss. Our arrangements for the night were not elaborate; we simply rolled ourselves up, each in his travelling rug, and went to sleep. There was no fear of cold or of sudden attack. Travellers in the African desert, or in the forests of the New World, are obliged to keep watch throughout the night; but here there was absolute solitude and safety. No savages or wild beasts would disturb us here.

We woke up refreshed, and went on, following the lava flow as before. It was impossible to tell what lay beyond the lava. The tunnel, instead of diving downwards, became absolutely horizontal. Indeed, it seemed to me that it was rising, and by ten o'clock in the morning I was sure of it. I was becoming exhausted and began to lag.

'Come along, Axel!' said the professor impatiently.

'But, Uncle, I can't keep up.'

'What! After three hours' easy walking!'

'It's not difficult, but it's very tiring,' I said.

'What! You find it tiring to go downhill!'

'Uphill, I should call it.'

'Uphill! What nonsense!' the professor snapped.

'Uphill of course,' I said. 'For the last half-hour the slopes have altered, and if we go on like this we shall certainly come back to earth.'

The professor shook his head angrily, like a man who will not listen to reason. I tried to persuade him, but he did not answer and gave the signal to go on. I could see that he was in a towering rage.

I shouldered my pack again, and followed as fast as I could. I did not want to be left behind; I was terrified at the thought of losing my way in this underground labyrinth. The uphill way was even steeper, but I consoled myself with the hope that we should soon be back on the surface of the earth again. Each step made me more certain.

About noon I noticed a change in the walls of the gallery. They no longer gave dazzling reflections from our electric lamps; they were no longer made of lava but of various other sorts of rock. In my excitement I started talking to myself.

'These are rocks formed by ancient seas,' I said, 'they're chalk and limestone; we're certainly going a very long way round, if we want to reach the centre of the earth!'

'What's that?' said my uncle, overhearing.

'Only that we've reached the rocks formed in the times of the first plant and animal life.'

'You think so?'

'Look for yourself!' I forced the professor to shine his lamp on the walls. He looked, but he said not a word and began walking on again.

Could he have understood? Was he too obstinate to confess his mistake in choosing the eastern tunnel, or was he determined to follow it to the end? Then I began to wonder whether I might not have been mistaken myself. But no, I had been right, the rock walls were full of all sorts of vegetable and animal fossils. At last I picked up a complete fossil shell and handed it to him.

'Look at that!' I said.

'Well, Axel,' he said calmly, 'it's the shell of a crustacean of the extinct order of trilobites. That's what.'

'But, then, don't you agree . . .'

'Yes, certainly. I agree that we have left the volcanic rock behind. I may have made a mistake, but I shan't be quite certain until we reach the end of this tunnel.'

'I admire your thoroughness, Uncle, but we're going to run out of water very soon.'

'Very well. We'll ration our water.'

19

A Mine with no Miners

It was certainly very necessary to ration our water; at supper that evening I realised that we had only enough for three days. And there was little hope of finding a spring in rock beds of that particular nature.

During the whole of the following day, the gallery stretched before us with its interminable arcades. We walked in an almost Icelandic silence. The path was not uphill, or not noticeably so, and sometimes it seemed even to be going downhill. But the nature of the rock beds remained the same. The lamplight sparkled on crystals in the limestone and showed up the old red sandstone of the walls; we might have been in the heart of Devonshire. In some places there were blocks of magnificent marble, some of agate-grey with white veins, others crimson, or yellow stained with red blotches, or dark brown.

The fossils were no longer of the most primitive forms of life, but now included fishes and early reptiles. We were climbing back up the scale of life. But Professor Lidenbrock did not seem to be worried; he was probably expecting either to come to a vertical shaft which would allow us to go downwards again, or to be stopped short by the end of the passage. But when the evening came we were still in the same seemingly endless gallery.

On Friday, after a night during which I began to feel the torments of thirst, our little band marched on again. After ten hours' walking, I noticed that the walls had grown very dark. The tunnel became extremely narrow, and I leaned against the wall. When I looked at my hand, it was quite black. I examined the tunnel more closely.

'A coal-mine!' I cried.

'A mine with no miners,' said my uncle.

'Who knows?' I said.

'I know,' said the professor shortly. 'I'm quite sure that no human hand hewed out this gallery. But what does it matter? It's supper time; let's eat.'

Hans prepared some food. I ate very little, and drank the few drops of water which made up my ration. The guide's flask half full was all that remained for three. The others lay down and seemed to drop off peacefully after their meal; but I could not sleep; I counted the hours till morning.

At six on Saturday we set off again. Twenty minutes later we reached a vast cavern; then I realised that this coal-mine could not be the work of man, the vaults would have been propped up. It was a miracle that they had not fallen in.

We walked on, and I tried to forget my thirst by thinking of the wonderful formation of coal from the tropical forests of ancient times. I was very glad, too, that we had our electric lamps, because I could smell a strong odour of marsh gas, which is highly inflammable and has caused some appalling catastrophes. If we had gone into that atmosphere with a naked flame, a terrific explosion would have put an end to our story.

We went on through the coal-mine till evening. My uncle was beside himself with frustration, and I was beginning to think that there was no end to the passage, when suddenly at six o'clock we came up against a blank wall. There was no way out, either right or left, above or below.

'Good,' said my uncle, 'now we know. We're not on Saknussemm's route, and we must return. We'll get a night's rest now, then in three days we'll be back at the fork in the road.'

'Yes,' I said, 'if we have the strength.'

'And why not?'

'Because tomorrow our water will be all gone.'

'And our courage too?' said the professor with a fierce look. I was cowed.

Just then Hans reminded my uncle that it was Saturday, and pay-day.

20

Thirst

I will not dwell on the nightmare journey back. My uncle was angry because he had made a mistake; I was in misery and despair; only Hans was completely calm and resigned.

Our water gave out at the end of the first day. We had nothing but neat gin, which burnt the gullet, so that I could not bear even the sight of it. It was very hot, I was exhausted, and more than once I stumbled and would never have got to my feet again without the comfort and support of Hans and my uncle. But the professor was in a pretty bad way himself.

At last, on Tuesday, 7th July, crawling on all fours, we dragged ourselves half-dead to the crossroads. Hans and my uncle tried to nibble a few crumbs of biscuit, but I sank to the ground, and lay there groaning, with swollen lips. I must have lost consciousness completely because the next thing I knew was that my uncle was bending over me, holding my head in his arms, and murmuring, 'Poor boy!'

My astonishment at hearing these words, in a tone of real tenderness, from my fierce uncle, must have shocked me back to life. Then he put the flask to my lips, saying, 'Drink.'

I thought he must be delirious.

'Drink,' he repeated. He tipped up the flask and emptied it into my mouth. Oh joy! A mouthful of water slaked my burning mouth – only one, but it was enough to save me.

'Just a drop,' he said. 'I kept it for you. It was a temptation, though, I must confess.'

The few drops of water had eased the torment of my thirst. I could speak again, I tried to thank my uncle, but he brushed my words aside.

'Now,' he said, 'let's go on.'

I was aghast. I had been quite sure that now he would be willing to give up the whole mad plan, and I tried to persuade him to retrace our path and climb up to the crater of Snaefells again. If we ever had the strength to do that we should be able to slake our thirst at last with snow.

But he was utterly determined to go through with it to the end. He told me that I was perfectly free to return, and Hans with me, but that for his part, he would never abandon his quest. I was almost at my wits' end. I tried to persuade Hans to return with me, but he simply shook his head very gently and, pointing to my uncle, said, 'Master.'

I tried to force Hans to leave my uncle, whom I believed to be quite mad. But it was useless, the Icelander sat there like a faithful hound and refused to budge.

'Pull yourself together, Axel,' said my uncle. 'You'll never get him to leave me. Now listen, I have a proposition.'

I folded my arms and looked him in the face.

'The only obstacle to my plans is lack of water,' he said. 'We had bad luck with the eastern tunnel; it's possible that we shall have better luck with the other.'

I shook my head.

'Hear me out,' he went on. 'While you were lying there, I had a look in the other passage. I think it goes right down into the earth, and that very soon we'll come to the granite, which will be full of springs. This is what I propose: when Columbus asked his sick and terrified crew for three days, they gave in and agreed to his demand, and he discovered America. Now I am the Columbus of this underground world, and I ask you for only *one* day. If at the end of that one day we haven't found water, I'll give in, I swear, and we'll go back.'

I was persuaded against my will by the strength of his passion. 'All right,' I said. 'As you like. I agree to your one day.'

21

The Search for Water

We started down the western tunnel, with Hans in front, as usual. After a hundred paces or so, the professor, shining his lamp on the walls, cried out:

'This is primitive rock! This is the right way! Come on!'

We were in a crack in the volcanic granite. At times the walls shone green, with bright metallic threads of copper and manganese, and with traces of gold and platinum. Then there was gneiss in layers and mica in shining flakes. As the light picked out the facets of the mica in fiery sparks, I felt as if I were making my way through a hollow diamond, so brilliant were the reflected rays.

About six in the evening, the light grew dimmer; the walls were darker, though still crystalline. We were in a vast prison of granite.

By eight o'clock I was exhausted, tortured by thirst. My uncle would not stop; his ears were strained to catch any murmur of water. But there was nothing.

At last I fell, with a cry of utter despair. My uncle was forced to stop; it was the end of his one day, the end of his hopes.

He stood over me with folded arms.

'It's the end,' he said. I shut my eyes against his glare of fury.

When I looked up again, I saw my two companions rolled in their blankets. Were they asleep? I could not tell, and it was impossible for me to sleep. We should certainly never have the strength to return to earth again, we should die there under the weight of the granite crust of the earth like rats in a trap. I felt that life was utterly crushed out of me.

Some hours passed. The granite tunnel was as silent as a tomb, and soon it would become our tomb indeed. No sound came through these walls, of which the thinnest was five miles thick.

Then suddenly I seemed to hear a noise; I tried to look through the darkness, and I thought I saw Hans slipping away with a lamp in his hand. I had a moment of terror. 'Hans is quitting,' I thought, and then I was ashamed that I should even for a moment have suspected that faithful man. He was certainly going somewhere, but he was going *down* the gallery, not up it. There could be only one reason for this. In the silence of the night he must have heard some murmur inaudible to my ears.

22

Hans Finds Water

I lay there for an hour or more, almost delirious in my excitement, my head filled with fantastic ideas. I was no longer sure whether I was in my right mind.

At last I heard footsteps. Hans was coming back. A faint light flickered along the walls, then Hans appeared. He went up to my uncle, and putting a hand on his shoulder, he wakened him gently. My uncle sat up.

'What is it?' he said.

'*Vatten*,' replied the guide.

'Water, water!' I cried.

'Water!' said my uncle. '*Hvar?*' he asked Hans.

'*Nedat*,' said Hans.

Down below – I understood that, and gripped the guide's hand in my excitement. He gave me a quiet smile.

We flung our things together and soon we were scrambling down the steep corridor. About an hour later we distinctly heard an unaccustomed sound running along in the gigantic walls, a sort of heavy rumbling like distant thunder. During our feverish journey I was almost overcome with the agony of my parched and burning mouth and throat. Then suddenly my uncle said:

'It's true! Hans was right! That noise is the sound of water! There's a subterranean river somewhere near us!'

We rushed along, frantic with hope. I no longer felt tired, the sound of water had given me new strength. We could hear the roaring of the torrent in the left-hand wall; often I touched it, hoping to find it damp, but it was perfectly dry.

We had been following the sound of the water for half an hour, and I realised that Hans could not have gone beyond this point. He had smelt the water through the rock, like a water-diviner, but he could not have tasted or even seen it. And now, to our disappointment, the sound of the stream was not so loud; we were evidently going away from it. We turned, and Hans stopped at the point which he judged to be nearest to the water.

I sat down by the wall, listening to the torrent raging beyond the granite, and it was almost too much for me. Were we to die of thirst after all, within sound of water?

Hans was looking at me and I thought he smiled slightly. Then he took up the lamp, and listened with his ear pressed to the wall. At last he found what he thought was the best place, about three feet above the ground.

My uncle and I exchanged glances, our hopes rising again. We could see what Hans was going to do. Of course it was desperately dangerous – to attack the granite wall with a pick. There might be a fall of rock which would smash us to smithereens, or we might be swept away by the mighty torrent of the subterranean river. But our plight was so desperate that any risk was justified.

If my uncle or I had tried to breach the wall, we would have been far too violent and probably caused a disaster. But Hans set to work like a stone-mason or a sculptor, with a rain of little blows on the same place, very calm and steady. He was making a hole about six inches across, and already the noise of the water was louder.

After an hour's work the pick had made a hole about two feet deep. It was agonising to wait. I had to restrain my uncle by force, and he had already caught up his pick to lend a hand, which would probably have been fatal, when suddenly there was a hissing sound. A jet of water shot right across the tunnel and drenched the opposite wall.

Hans was nearly felled by the force of the water, and could not control a cry of pain. I understood why when I touched the jet and at once sprang back – also with a cry: the water was boiling.

'It'll cool down,' said the professor, who had prudently kept out of the way of the jet. The tunnel filled with steam, while the water turned into a little river and flowed away down our path. Soon we were able to drink. The pleasure of that moment, when the water first filled our mouths and flowed down our throats, cannot be described; no one could understand it unless he too had almost died of thirst. The water was still hot when we began to gulp it, lying full length on the floor of the tunnel and drinking eagerly as if we could never be filled.

At last I raised my head, and then I realised what a strange taste it had.

'It tastes of iron!' I said.

'Excellent for the stomach,' said my uncle. 'People pay a lot of money at health resorts to drink water like this.'

'How good it is!'

'It's got an inky flavour, not at all disagreeable. I think we must christen it after Hans, who discovered it.' So we named it the Hansbrook. Hans himself did not seem particularly impressed by his new glory. After drinking his moderate fill he had sat down quietly in a corner.

'Now,' I said, 'don't you think we'd better take care not to let all this water run away?'

'I should have thought,' answered the professor, 'that the river was inexhaustible.'

'I think we ought to fill the goatskin and the flasks, then stop up the hole.'

My uncle agreed, so Hans tried to stop the hole with granite chips and tow. But it was impossible, he scalded his hands to no purpose.

'Don't you think it would be a better idea,' said my uncle, 'since in any case we can't stop it up, to take advantage of this stream? It will flow along beside us and give us as much water as we want. No need to burden ourselves with water on our backs when the ground will bear it for us.'

This idea seemed to me quite brilliant, and I wondered why I had not thought of it myself. I was even preparing to start off again immediately, in the happy companionship of the stream. But my uncle stopped me.

'It's too late tonight,' he said. 'We'll get a few hours' sleep, and then we'll start refreshed tomorrow.'

23

Journey Under the Earth

When I woke in the morning I felt an extraordinary sense of well-being. I could not understand it at first, till I heard the stream murmuring at my feet. We ate our breakfast and drank the wonderful iron-tasting water. I was on top of the world – that is, in my mind! Nothing could beat us now, we three were going to make history.

'Let's get started!' I cried, in a voice that made the echoes ring down that corridor which had been silent since the creation of the earth.

On Thursday at eight in the morning we set off again. The granite passage twisted and turned in mazy wanderings, but the general direction was always to the south-east. My uncle kept his eye on the compass, and took notes all the time. The path was almost horizontal with only a very slight downward slope, with the stream running along gently beside us all the way.

The companionship of the water made me cheerful, but the levelness of the path enraged my uncle. The way to the centre was enormously increased by the slightness of the slope, but we had no choice. Every now and again, however, the downward slopes did become steeper and put my uncle in a rather better temper. Altogether, that day and the next, we made good forward progress but very little in depth.

On Friday evening, 10th July, we estimated that we were about ninety miles south-east of Reykjavik and almost eight miles deep. Then suddenly we came to the mouth of an alarming shaft in the rock bed. My uncle clapped his hands with delight.

'Now at last we can get on!' he cried. 'And look – the jutting rocks make an easy staircase.'

Hans arranged the ropes, in his usual workmanlike way, and the descent began. The shaft was a sort of narrow crack in the granite, a geological fault, caused by the shrinking of the earth's crust as it cooled. If it had once served as a channel for molten rock during eruptions, there was now no trace of any volcanic material. We were climbing down a sort of spiral stairway which might almost have been made by the hand of man.

Every quarter of an hour we had to rest to ease the strain on our ankles. We would sit on a projecting rock, with dangling legs, eating, talking, and drinking from the stream. It was a waterfall now, dashing down from rock to rock. If the Hansbrook was a good name while it was running peacefully along its almost level bed, it should now have been rechristened after my violent uncle Otto.

On 11th and 12th July we followed the steep spirals of the fault, diving six miles farther down into the earth, so that we were now about fifteen miles below sea level. But on the 13th, about noon, the fault took a slighter angle, about forty-five degrees, still leading towards the south-east.

With this, the path became easy and extremely boring, as was only to be expected, since there was no variety of landscape as on an overland journey.

On Wednesday 15th we were twenty-one miles down and about a hundred and fifty miles from Snaefells. Although we were rather tired we were in good health, and we had not touched our medicine-chest. My uncle kept an hourly check by means of the compass, the chronometer, the manometer and the thermometer, keeping observations which he has since published in his scientific account of the journey. When he told me that we had travelled a hundred and fifty miles horizontally, I had rather a shock.

'What's the matter?' he asked.

'Nothing – only, if you're right, we're no longer under Iceland!'

'Well?'

'I'll make sure.' I consulted the map and the compass. 'Yes, as I thought, we've passed Cape Portland and are now under the open sea.'

'Well, why not?' said my uncle, rubbing his hands. 'There are coal-mines at Newcastle which stretch out under the sea.'

The professor took it quite calmly, but I was a little worried at the thought of the mass of the ocean over our heads. But after all, it hardly mattered whether we were under the Icelandic mountains or the Atlantic waves, as long as the rock held up. I became gradually used to the idea as we followed the granite corridor, which was all the time leading us down into the depths.

Three days later, on Saturday, 18th July, in the evening, we came to a sort of vast cavern. My uncle gave Hans his weekly wages of three rixdollars, and it was decided that the next day, Sunday, should be a day of rest.

24

Scientific Arguments Under the Ocean

I woke up that Sunday morning with the pleasant sensation that we did not have to dash off. I lay there in my blanket, enjoying our troglodyte life. I hardly missed the sun, the stars, the moon, the trees, the houses or the towns – all those earthly things which had once seemed so necessary to me. I was a fossil, no longer interested in these useless marvels.

The grotto was like a huge hall; the faithful stream ran gently along on the granite floor. It had now cooled down to the temperature of the surrounding air and could be drunk at will.

After a leisurely breakfast, the professor set himself to put his notes in order. He spread out his instruments and his notebooks on a convenient slab of granite, found a smaller piece of rock for a seat, and set to work. I sat beside him on another rock on which I had folded my blanket for greater comfort.

'Now, Axel,' he said, as if he were beginning one of our sessions in his study at home. 'First of all I want to calculate our exact position, so that when we get back I can make a map of our journey, a sort of vertical section of the earth which will give our route in profile.'

'That will be very interesting, Uncle, but are your notes accurate enough?'

'Yes. I have observed the angles and the slopes with scrupulous accuracy; I have certainly made no mistakes. First, let's see where we are. Take the compass and give me our direction.'

I looked at the compass and gave him the reading, it was almost due east-south-east.

'Good!' said the professor, jotting down the observation and making some quick calculations. 'We have come two hundred and fifty-five miles from our starting-point.'

'So we're under the Atlantic?'

'Exactly.'

'And perhaps, at this very moment, there's a storm, and ships are going down over our heads?'

'It's perfectly possible.'

'And maybe there are huge whales striking their tails against the walls of our prison?'

'Don't fret, Axel, they won't knock them down. Let's get on. We are two hundred and fifty-five miles south-east of Snaefells, and forty-eight miles deep, according to my calculations.'

'But that's about the thickness of the earth's crust, according to scientists.'

'I dare say.'

'Well, then, Uncle, according to all the rules, it ought to be one thousand five hundred degrees Centigrade[1] down here!'

'So it ought, my dear boy.'

'And all this granite should be in a state of flux!'

[1] 2732°F.

'That's what comes of theory, when you test it by practice!'

'I suppose I must agree, but it's very strange and rather upsetting for a young student who has only just learnt all the theory!'

'What does the thermometer say?' said my uncle.

'27·6 degrees.'[1]

'Well, there you are then,' said my uncle, gleefully rubbing his hands. 'Don't believe all you read in the books. What have you got to say to that?'

'Nothing,' I said. But really I could have said a great deal, only I knew too well that it was useless to argue with my uncle. I still believed that there was a central furnace in the earth, only it seemed to me that we were insulated from the heat by a sort of coating of lava. However, I let it go at that, and took up another point.

'I'm sure your calculations are accurate, Uncle,' I went on, 'but I've been thinking – do you agree that at this latitude the radius of the earth is about 4749 miles?'

'4750.'

'Call it 4800 in round numbers. And of that, we have done forty-eight miles, or one-hundredth?'

'As you say.'

'And in twenty days, on a diagonal course?' I persisted.

'Of course.'

'Then if we go on at this rate, we shall take two thousand days, or about five and a half years, to reach the centre!'

The professor said nothing; he was glaring at me, but I went boldly on:

[1] 82°F.

'And there's something else – if we have to go two hundred and fifty miles horizontally for every fifty miles vertically, more or less, then we're bound to come out somewhere on the circumference long before we reach the centre!'

'To hell with your calculations!' screamed the professor. 'How do you know we'll go on at the same rate? You forget that we're not the first – a man has already done it, and if he succeeded, I shall succeed too!'

'I hope so, Uncle, but if I may be allowed—'

'Allowed nothing! You can hold your tongue, Axel, if you can't talk more sense!'

So I held my tongue.

'Now consult the manometer,' he said coldly. 'What does it indicate?'

'A considerable pressure.'

'There, you see,' he went on, almost in his usual professorial tones. 'By going down gradually, we have grown used to the increased pressure, and feel no ill effects.'

'None at all, except that I've got earache.'

'You're not going to make a fuss about a little earache, I hope. Breathe quickly and deeply, and it will soon pass.'

'Yes, Uncle,' I said meekly. 'Have you noticed how clearly sounds are heard at this depth?'

'Yes, I have – even a deaf man could hear.'

'I suppose the density of the air will increase?' I asked.

'Certainly, and of course our weight will decrease as we go deeper.'

'And in the end,' I said, 'the air will be as dense as water?'

'Yes, and even denser, as we go still farther down.'

'Then how shall we be able to go down? We shall surely

float when the air becomes as thick as oil!'

'Well, we'll just have to fill our pockets with stones.'

He had an answer to everything; but in the end we should come to the point where the air was completely solid, and then not even Professor Lidenbrock would be able to force his way through it.

It was no good arguing with him, he would only have answered all my objections with the example of his everlasting Saknussemm. I had a very simple answer to that. In the sixteenth century neither the barometer nor the manometer had been invented; how then had Saknussemm known that he had reached the centre of the earth?

But I kept this argument to myself.

25

I Lose My Way

Things were really going very well, and I even began to be almost as hopeful as my uncle that we would succeed in the end, and win great glory. Perhaps it was the strange atmosphere of that underground journey.

Sometimes for days on end we were climbing down almost vertically, at certain times we made five or six miles depth in a single day. There were some very tricky places; if it had not been for Hans, his skill and his extraordinary coolness and presence of mind, we should never have come through.

During these perilous climbs we hardly spoke at all. I am sure that surroundings have a strong effect on the brain; I believe that a man shut up alone within four walls ends by losing the power of speech. We had each other's company, but we felt tiny and very isolated in these subterranean chasms.

For two weeks after our last scientific conversation, nothing happened worthy of note. Then came an adventure which I shall never forget.

By 7th August we were about ninety miles down, and about six hundred miles from Iceland. The tunnel was sloping gradually downwards; I was in front, with one of the electric lamps, while my uncle had the other. I was examining the granite beds.

Suddenly I looked round and found myself alone.

'Well,' I thought, 'I've been going too fast, or they must have stopped somewhere. I'll go back. Luckily the slope is not too steep.'

I walked back for a quarter of an hour or so. No one to be seen. I called. No reply. Only the echoes of my own voice mocked me down the hollow path. A cold fear pricked my spine.

'Keep quite calm,' I said to myself aloud. 'They can't be far. I was in front, I can't miss them, if I go straight back. There's only the one path.'

I kept on walking back. I listened, in case they were calling me, but the gallery was strangely silent. I stopped. I could not believe I was really lost; I had just missed my way, I should certainly find the others before long.

'There's only the one path,' I repeated to myself, 'they must be somewhere along it; if I keep on going back I'm bound to run into them. Unless they've forgotten that I was in front, and have turned back themselves to look for me. Even so, if I hurry, I'll catch them up. It stands to reason!'

It stands to reason. The words sounded hollow. Had I really been in front? But of course; Hans was behind me, then my uncle. I remembered clearly looking back and seeing Hans fiddling with the strap of his pack which had worked loose. It was the last thing I remembered before stepping forward again.

'Never mind,' I thought, 'I've only to follow the stream back up its bed, and I'll find them sooner or later.' I felt that a wash and a drink would do me good, and I stooped to plunge my head in the waters of the Hansbrook.

The whole floor of the tunnel was nothing but dry rock. There was no stream.

26

Lost

It was a horrible moment. I was buried alive, and I should soon die of hunger and thirst.

How had I lost the stream? Now I understood why the gallery had seemed so strangely silent when I had listened for any sound from the others. I must at some point have taken a wrong turning, away from the course of the murmuring water.

How was I to find my way back? My feet had left no marks on the granite floor. I was lost – lost ninety miles below the surface of the earth. I thought of my home, and my sweetheart whom I would never see again, and I was in utter despair.

The black moment passed. I began to consider my situation as calmly as I could. I had food for three days, and my flask was full. It was clear to me that I must climb back upwards, towards the fork in the path where I must have gone wrong. If I could only find the stream of water, I could eventually retrace my path to Snaefells again.

I started back, leaning on my steel-tipped stick. The path was fairly steep but I was full of hope. I tried to recognise the route by means of particular rocks, but they all looked alike to me. Then suddenly I knew I had gone wrong: I had come to a dead end.

I was overwhelmed with terror and despair; my last hope smashed against that granite wall. I was lost in a maze of winding paths, I should soon die a lonely death. Yet even in the depths of my misery, I had a whimsical thought – that if my fossilised bones should ever be discovered, ninety miles below the surface of the earth, the scientists of the future would have something to scratch their heads about!

I tried to cry aloud but my terror had taken away the power of speech; I could do nothing but groan between dry lips.

Worse was to come. I had dropped my lamp in my panic, and now its light was failing. I had no tools to repair it; I could only watch the luminous filament growing faint. I dared not take my eyes from it, fearing to lose the last gleam of light. When in the end it went out I gave a terrible cry. I was in absolute darkness. On the earth, even on the darkest nights, there is always a little glimmer, the sky is never completely black. But here, there was no light at all. I was blind.

At that moment I lost my head. I jumped up, stretching out my arms, and groped painfully along the wall; I began to run helter-skelter through the subterranean maze; I was running downhill, away from the surface of the earth, crying, howling, screaming, tearing my hands against sharp rocks, falling headlong and rising with blood streaming down my face, licking the blood, expecting always to run head first against a wall and dash out my doomed life.

I had no longer the faintest idea where I was, and at last I dropped in utter exhaustion, and lost consciousness.

27

Voices in the Dark

When I recovered my senses, my face was wet with tears. I had no idea how long I had been lying there, I had no means of telling the time. No prisoner in solitary confinement was ever more alone than I.

After falling, I had lost a lot of blood. I felt myself sticky with it. I wished that I had already died and that I did not have to face death any more. I lay down by the wall, and made my mind a blank. I was already beginning to sink into a coma, and this time it would have been fatal. Then suddenly I was roused by a violent noise like thunder, which rolled away in echoes down the distant vaults of my prison. I supposed that the noise must be due to some natural cause, the explosion of some gas or a heavy fall of rock. As I listened, the echoes died away, and silence was renewed in the gallery. Even the beating of my heart seemed to have ceased.

Then by chance I pressed my ear against the wall, and I seemed to hear the sound of voices – vague, indistinct, faraway. I trembled.

'It's a mirage of sound!' I thought. But no. I listened very hard, and I did really hear a murmur of voices, though I was too weak to understand what was said.

I had a moment of fear that the words were my own, brought back by some trick of the echoes. I might have spoken aloud without realising it. I shut my lips tight and glued my ear to the wall. The voices were really there! I dragged myself a little further along the wall, and found I could hear more clearly. There was a murmuring of low voices, with the word '*förlorad*' repeated several times in tones of sorrow.

Then if I could hear them, they must be able to hear me too!

'Help! Help!' I cried at the top of my voice.

I listened, straining my ears, but no one answered. But it must be my uncle and Hans, it could not possibly be anyone else. I began listening again, moving along the wall till I found the point where the voices sounded loudest. I heard the word '*förlorad*' again, then the thunder-roll which had aroused me from my coma. It occurred to me that the voices did not come through the granite wall, but along the gallery, by some peculiar acoustic effect.

I listened again, and this time I distinctly heard my own name! I realised then that the wall acted as a kind of conductor of sound, and that to be heard, I must throw my voice along the gallery. But I had no time to lose: if they moved, we should probably lose the acoustic connection. So I went close up to the wall, and called, as clearly as I could:

'Uncle Otto!' I waited in an agony of suspense. Sound does not travel very fast, and the increased density of the air could not speed it up, it could only make it louder. A few seconds passed, though they felt like ages, then I heard these words:

'Axel! Axel! Is that you?'

111

'Yes! Yes!' I answered.

'My poor boy, where are you?'
'Lost in utter darkness!'

'What about your lamp?'
'Out!'

'And the stream?'
'Vanished!'

'Axel, poor Axel, be brave!'
'Wait . . . I'm all in . . . I can't talk . . . but talk to me!'

'Right!' said my uncle. 'Listen! We searched for you all up and down the gallery. We thought you'd be somewhere along the course of the stream, so we walked along it, firing shots. Now at least we can speak to each other – that's always something – don't lose heart!'

While I listened, I was thinking hard. I had a ray of hope.

'Uncle!' I said, speaking close to the wall.

'Yes, Axel?' came the reply after a few seconds.
'We must find out how far apart we are.'

'That's easy, I have my chronometer.'
'All right, look at it and call my name, noting the exact second. As soon as I hear it, I'll repeat it, and you must note the exact second my voice reaches you.'

'Good, and half the time between my call and your reply will tell us what we want to know. Are you ready?'

'Yes, ready!' I held my ear to the wall, and as soon as I caught the sound 'Axel' I replied? 'Axel,' and waited.

'Forty seconds!' said my uncle. 'That means twenty seconds from you to me. At 1020 feet per second, that makes 20,400 feet, or about four miles.'

'Four miles!' I gasped.

'That's not too bad, Axel!'

'But which way – up or down?'

'Down – I'll tell you why. We're in a vast cavern, with a great number of passages leading down into it. Follow *down* the one you're in, and you'll find us, since I'm sure that all these cracks fan out round the cave where we are. Pick yourself up, drag yourself along, slide down the steep places, you'll find us waiting for you. Come along – we'll see you soon!'

His words gave me strength. 'All right, Uncle,' I said, 'I'm starting now – I shan't be able to speak again, goodbye!'

'Soon – see you soon!'

I set off, thanking God from my heart that I had found the one place, perhaps, where our words could reach each other through all this black immensity. I remembered what I had read of the Whispering Gallery in the dome of St Paul's Cathedral in London, and of those old quarries at Syracuse in Sicily, particularly the one called the Ear of Dionysus. Then I realised that there could be no obstacle between my uncle and me, since the sound had been able to travel for four miles, so that in the end I was bound to reach him, if I only kept going.

I dragged myself along, and then as the slope became steeper, I let myself slide. Steeper and steeper grew the the path; I had not the strength to hold myself back, it was like a chute at a fair, but hard and rough. Suddenly the ground gave way under my feet. I felt myself roll bouncing down the rugged sides of a vertical shaft, like a well; my head hit a sharp rock and I lost consciousness.

28

Saved!

When I came to myself it was not completely dark, and I felt soft rugs under me. My uncle's face was bent over me. He saw my eyes open and took my hand with a delighted cry.

'He's alive!' he said.

'Yes!' I gasped.

'My *dear* boy!' he said, almost in tears. Then Hans appeared, and seeing my eyes open, he smiled.

'*God dag!*' he said.

'And a very good day to you too,' I murmured. 'Tell me, Uncle, where are we?'

'Tomorrow, Axel, no more excitement now; your head is swathed in compresses and you must sleep now.'

'But at least tell me the time.'

'It's eleven at night; it's Sunday, 9th August; no more questions tonight.'

So I had been lost for three days! With that thought I dropped off to sleep again.

When I woke in the morning, I looked round me. My bed, made up of our entire supply of travelling-rugs, was in a beautiful cave, adorned with fine stalagmites and floored with sand. It was not quite dark, and yet no lamp was lit. A strange radiance streamed through a narrow opening into the cave. I became aware also of a vague murmur like the sound of waves breaking on a beach, and sometimes I seemed to hear the wind.

At first I thought I must be dreaming, or that my brain had been affected by my fall, and I was hearing imaginary sounds. And yet everything seemed real enough. I thought then that we must by some strange means have returned to the surface of the earth while I slept.

The professor appeared.

'Good morning, Axel,' he said cheerfully. 'You're better, aren't you?'

'Yes, I am, much better,' I answered, sitting up.

'You slept well, I know, for Hans and I took turns watching you.'

'I'm a new man,' I said, 'and very hungry. Can I have some breakfast?'

'Of course you may, now your fever has gone. Hans has been rubbing your wounds with some secret Icelandic oint-ment, and they're already beginning to heal. One thing, though, don't eat too much at first!'

While he spoke he was bringing me food, which I ate ravenously, in spite of his warning. As I ate, I plied him with questions. I learnt that I had slipped down an almost perpen-dicular shaft, and had arrived in the middle of a shower of rocks of which the smallest would have crushed me. They therefore supposed that I had come down on top of a fall of rock, which had delivered me, unconscious and bleeding, into my uncle's arms.

'I can't think,' he said, 'how you weren't killed a hundred times over. Now we must never get separated again.'

What could he mean? Was the journey still unfinished? I looked at him with wide eyes, and he asked me what was the matter.

'Tell me, Uncle, am I really safe and sound?'

'Of course you are.'

'Have I all my limbs intact?'

'Certainly you have.'

'What about my head?'

'Your head, except for a few bruises, is as it should be, in its place on your shoulders.'

'What about my brain?'

'What do you mean?'

'I thought we'd come back to the surface of the earth!'

'Certainly not!'

'Well then I must be mad. I can see daylight, I can hear the wind and the sea!'

'Is that all?' asked the professor calmly.

'Please explain!'

'I can't explain, because it's inexplicable; but you'll see, and you'll find out that there are more things in heaven and earth . . . and under the earth . . .'

'Let's go and see, then!' I said, starting to get up.

'No, Axel! The fresh air may be too much for you.'

'*Fresh air?*'

'There's rather a strong wind. I don't want you to risk going out, yet.'

'But I'm fine!'

'Patience, dear boy. You mustn't have a relapse, it would

hold us up, and I don't want to lose time, as the crossing may be rather long.'

'What on earth are you talking about?'

'Rest today, and tomorrow we shall embark.'

Embark! What could he mean? Was there a river, a lake, or a sea? Was there a ship riding at anchor in some underground harbour? I was terribly excited, my curiosity was making me ill. When my uncle saw this, he decided that it would be better to let me have my way. I dressed quickly, and wrapped myself in a blanket as an extra precaution.

29

The Subterranean Sea

At first I could see nothing; my eyes, unused to light, would not stay open. When I could see again, I was overcome with astonishment.

'The sea!' I cried.

'Yes,' said my uncle, 'the Lidenbrock Sea: I don't think anyone will dispute my claim to have discovered this sea, or my right to call it by my name.'

A huge sheet of water stretched out into the distance. The shore, scalloped into wide bays, was covered with fine golden sand, scattered with little shells of primitive creatures. The breaking waves made a sonorous murmur; the wind blew flakes of foam into my face. Behind the beach rose steep rocky cliffs, towering to immense heights. Some of them cut sharply across the beaches and formed capes and promontories against which the surf thundered. It was a real ocean, like the oceans of the earth, but terribly wild and lonely.

A strange light shone over this subterranean sea. Not the hot brilliance of the sun, nor the cool pale radiance of the moon; but a clear cold white light, brighter than moonlight, but not so steady. It was evidently caused by natural electricity.

The vault over our heads – the sky, if you like – seemed to be made of huge clouds, moving vapours capable of shedding torrents of rain. But at present the weather was fine. White lights flickered over the highest clouds, there were black shadows on their undersides, and sometimes bright rays like sunlight gleamed down between the clouds. But the light was cold, and the whole effect was desperately sad and melancholy. Beyond the clouds was no sky spangled with stars, but a heavy vault of granite whose weight seemed overpowering.

On the other hand, after an imprisonment of forty-four days in a narrow tunnel, it was delightful to fill our lungs with the salt wind from the sea.

'Do you feel up to a little walk?' said my uncle.

'That would be fine,' I answered.

But all the same, I was glad to take my uncle's arm as we set off along the beach. On the left were the piled-up rocks of the mighty cliffs, with innumerable waterfalls cascading down their sides. Some of these falls were hot, as we could tell from the steam rising from them. Among them was our faithful Hansbrook, finding its way down to the sea as if it had taken that course since the beginning of the world.

'We shall miss our Hansbrook,' I said with a sentimental sigh.

'We'll find plenty more,' said the professor ungratefully.

Just then we came round the corner of a high headland and an extraordinary sight met our eyes. About a hundred yards away was a thick forest of tall trees. But they were very strange trees, like neat, regular umbrellas; they did not sway in the wind, but stood motionless, like petrified cedars. I rushed towards them, quite forgetting my aches and bruises, wondering what sort of trees they could be. When we were under their shade I recognised them for what they were, in spite of their gigantic size.

'It's nothing but a forest of mushrooms,' said my uncle.

We wandered for a while under the thousands of giant mushrooms and toadstools; it was quite dark and terribly cold under their fleshy domes, and I was glad when we came out again on the shore. There were other vegetable growths as well as the fungus. A little further on we saw clumps of trees with foliage of different colours. They were easy to recognise, because they were monstrous versions of some of our common plants. Here were thickets of clubmoss a hundred feet high, gigantic horsetails, tree-ferns as tall as northern pines, and huge succulents with round forked stems and long fat leaves, covered with thick rank hairs.

'Astonishing, magnificent, splendid!' cried my uncle. 'Here is all the flora of the second period of the world – the period of transition. What a feast for a botanist!'

'A fantastic collection of antediluvian plants,' I said, 'a sort of greenhouse of specimens we've only known till now from fossils.'

'You're right, Axel, and it's not only a greenhouse, it's a natural history museum – look at all these bones scattered on the ground.'

I looked down. It was true, the shore was littered with gigantic bones like tree-trunks. I ran from one to another in my excitement.

'Here's the lower jaw of a Mastodon,' I cried, 'and look, a dinosaur's teeth, and here's the thigh-bone of a Megatherium, the greatest of them all. These beasts must have lived on this sea-shore once, in the shade of these prehistoric forests. Here are even complete skeletons. Now I wonder . . .'

'What do you wonder?' asked the professor.

'I wonder how they could have got here, under the primitive granite. There was no animal life before the secondary period, when sedimentary rocks were formed by floods.'

'You're quite right,' said my uncle. 'I can only suppose that some of those sedimentary rocks slipped down through a great gulf in the granite, which then became sealed by later movements of the earth's crust.'

'Perhaps,' I said. Then I had a disturbing thought. 'How do we know,' I went on, 'that some of these antediluvian monsters haven't survived to this day, in these subterranean caverns, and perhaps they're still hiding in the dark forests or behind these steep rocks?' I looked round fearfully, but could see no trace of life along the mournful shores.

As I was rather tired I went to sit down on the end of a headland, above the angry waves. A great bay stretched out in front of me, with a little natural harbour between sheltering rocks. There was a good anchorage in its calm waters for a brig and two or three schooners. I almost expected to see some ship come gliding out of the harbour mouth under full sail.

But we were the only living creatures in this underground world, and when the wind dropped it was as silent as a tomb. I looked towards the misty horizon, wondering whether we should ever reach the far shore. My uncle had no doubts.

After an hour or so we made our way back beside the sea till we came to our cave. The strangest thoughts were chasing round in my head as I fell asleep that night.

30

Hans Builds a Raft

The next morning I woke up feeling quite well again. Here we are at the sea-side, I thought, and what could be nicer than a swim? So I ran down to the water's edge and had a delightful dip. I came back to breakfast refreshed and with a healthy appetite.

Hans now proved himself an expert at camp cooking, as well as all his other talents. He had water and fire, so he made a sort of hot hash from our dried meat and biscuit, which made a pleasant change. Afterwards he gave us coffee, and no coffee had ever tasted so good to me before.

'Now,' said my uncle, jumping up, 'the tide's coming in, let's go and look at it.'

'Is there really a tide here?' I asked.

'Why not? I suppose this underground sea is subject to the same natural laws as the seas of the earth.'

We walked along the sand, watching the waves. They certainly seemed to be coming in.

'The tide will rise about ten feet, I think,' said my uncle with his air of wisdom. Of course he had had plenty of time to study the behaviour of the sea before I had arrived on the scene.

'It's wonderful!' I said, humouring him.

'Not wonderful, perfectly natural.'

'It seems wonderful to me,' I went on, 'that there should be seas and countries under the earth like this.'

'Uninhabited, though,' said the professor.

'How do you know? There may be new varieties of fish under these waters.'

'I haven't seen any,' said my uncle.

'I've a good mind to fix up a rod and find out.'

'No harm in that, Axel; it might even be very interesting.'

'Can you tell me where we are now, Uncle?'

'Horizontally we are 1050 miles from Iceland, within a mile or so.'

'And still making towards the south-east?'

'Yes, but there's a strange thing about the needle of the compass. Instead of dipping towards the pole, as it does in the northern hemisphere, it actually slopes upwards.'

'That means,' I said, 'that the magnetic pole must be somewhere between the surface of the earth and the point where we are now?'

'Exactly, and if we were right under the polar regions, the needle would point straight upwards. The pole is certainly not very deep below the surface.'

'Surely, Uncle, that's a new scientific discovery?'

'Certainly it is; and science is full of mistakes, but there's a saying that if you don't make mistakes you'll never make anything.'

'How deep are we now?'

'One hundred and five miles down.'

I looked at the map. 'So we're under the highlands of Scotland. The Grampians are above us with their snowy summits.'

The professor laughed. 'Yes, but I think these granite vaults will bear their weight.'

'I'm not afraid of the roof falling in,' I said, 'but what are your plans? Aren't we ever going home?'

'My dear boy, we've only just started – this is where it begins to get really exciting. First we're going to cross the sea.'

'How do you plan to manage that?'

'Not by swimming! I look forward to finding a new route to the centre, when we reach the further shore.'

'How wide do you suppose the sea is?'

'About a hundred miles, I should imagine.'

Of course he was only guessing; he could not possibly know.

'So we've no time to lose,' he went on, 'we've dallied long enough. Tomorrow we shall embark.'

I looked round hopefully, almost expecting to see a ship, but of course the sea was as empty as before.

'You don't believe me?' he asked. 'Listen!' Through the air came the sound of hammer blows. 'Hans is making a raft,' he explained at last, when he thought he had mystified me long enough. 'Let's go and see how he's getting on.'

We set off in the direction of the hammering, and when we had rounded the rocky height which buttressed the little natural harbour, we saw Hans at work. To my great surprise, there was a raft already half finished on the sand; it was made of beams of some kind of wood, and the ground was strewn with many planks and billets of all shapes and sizes. There was enough material to build a whole navy.

'What wood is this, Uncle?'

'Pine, fir, birch, all the conifers of the north, mineralised by the sea – fossil wood.'

'But I thought fossil wood was as heavy as stone?'

'Sometimes, but not always; this wood hasn't got to that stage yet. Look!' He threw a piece into the water; it sank, then bobbed up again and floated on the waves.

The raft was finished by the following evening. It was ten feet long by five feet wide, and the beams were lashed together with strong rope. When we launched it, it floated quietly in the harbour.

31

On the Subterranean Sea

On the morning of 13th August we rose early, eager to try our new craft.

The rigging consisted of a mast fashioned from two staves spliced together, a yard made from a third, and one of our rugs as a sail. We had plenty of ropes, and Hans had made a very seaworthy job.

By six o'clock we were ready to set sail. All our baggage – food and clothing, a good supply of fresh water in all our containers, instruments and firearms – was lashed into place.

Hans had made a rudder to steer by, so he took the helm, and the professor and I climbed aboard. I loosed the mooring-rope, the sail was set, and we pushed off. My uncle wanted to call the harbour after me, but I had another idea.

'Let's call it Port Gretel,' I said, 'that will look fine on the map.' So it was agreed.

There was a fair breeze blowing from the north-east; as soon as we had left the harbour behind we made good speed. After the first hour's sailing my uncle said:

'If we go on like this we'll make at least ninety miles in twenty-four hours and we'll soon be in sight of the further shores.'

I went to lie in the bows, if a raft has bows. Already the southern shore was sinking below the horizon. Before our eyes stretched the vast ocean, with grey cloud shadows moving over the surface. The silver rays of the electric light glittered on the water-drops which clung to the sides of the raft. Soon we lost sight of land, and the foamy wake of our craft was the only visible movement.

Towards noon the surface of the sea was covered with huge floating algae or seaweed. I knew how luxuriant the growth of seaweed can be, how it can form dense tangled beds and hold up the movement of ships, but there were never algae so gigantic as these in the Lidenbrock Sea. We sailed along beside enormous ribbons of weed like sea-serpents with no visible end. For hours I watched some of these ribbons, but still no end appeared.

Evening came, but no darkness. The sky stayed as light as ever. After supper I lay down beside the mast and fell asleep. Hans, motionless at the tiller, let the raft run before the wind, for there was no need to steer.

I was in charge of the log of this voyage. I had to keep detailed notes of any interesting phenomena, the direction of the wind, our speed, the distance covered, and anything else I could think of. Here is an extract from the log:

Friday, 14th August. Steady north-west wind. Raft sailing fast and straight. Coast about ninety miles to leeward. Nothing on the horizon. Continuous light. Fine clouds very high, thin and shining with a white light like molten silver. Thermometer: 32 degrees Centigrade.[1]

The rest of the account of our voyage is written up from my log.

At noon, Hans tied a hook to a line, baited it with a small piece of meat and cast it into the sea. For two hours nothing happened, then he had a bite. He hauled in the line and landed a fish which flapped about wildly on the raft.

'A sturgeon!' I cried. 'A little sturgeon!'

The professor examined our catch. He did not agree with me about the kind of fish; it had a flat, round head, the fore part of its body was covered with bony plates, it had no teeth, and there were fins but no tail. It was of the sturgeon family, but different from the sturgeons we knew.

My uncle looked up and said: 'This fish belongs to a family which has been extinct for centuries; we find fossil remains of it in the Devonian strata.'

'This is very exciting,' I said, 'do you mean we've really taken an extinct fish alive?'

'We have indeed; it's a thrill for a naturalist!'

'What family does it belong to?' I asked.

'To the order of Ganoids, family of Cephalaspides, genus . . .' he hesitated. 'Genus Pterychtis, I'm fairly sure, but there's a peculiarity about it, no doubt because it lives in subterranean waters . . .'

'What's that?'

'It's blind, and not only that, but it has no trace of eyes.'

[1] 90°F.

We baited the line and cast it again. In two hours we took a large quantity of Pterychtis, and some fish of another extinct race, the Dipterides. None of them had any eyes. This unexpected haul made a welcome addition to our food supply.

So the sea was full of extinct fish, as the land of extinct plants! I began to wonder whether we might not meet some of those prehistoric reptiles which are known only through their fossil remains. I took the telescope and scanned the sea. It was deserted; no doubt we were still too near the shore.

Then I looked upwards, hoping to catch a glimpse of one of the first birds: there would be plenty of fish to feed them. But the sky was empty of life.

However, my imagination peopled the underground world with all those extinct monsters I had seen reconstructed in museums. I thought I saw enormous Chersites, those ante-diluvian turtles, like floating islands. I felt that the dark groves of the shore were alive with the first mammals: the Leptotherium, found in Brazilian caves, the Lericotherium, from the frozen Siberian wastes. Further on, the Lophiodon, a gigantic tapir, was lurking behind the rocks, ready to fight to the death over its prey with the Anoplotherium, that strange beast akin to the rhinoceros, the horse, the hippopotamus and the camel together – as if the Creator during the rush of the first days of creation had made several animals into one. The mighty Mammoth waved his trunk and shattered the rocks with his tusks, while the Megatherium, crouching on enormous paws, rootled in the earth and woke echoes from the granite cliffs with his bellowing. Higher up, the first ape, or Protopithecus, climbed the steep mountain-tops, and above him the Pterodactyl with its winged hands glided like a giant bat in the dense air. Highest of all, immense birds, more powerful than the cassowary, larger than the ostrich, spread their vast wings and grazed the granite roof with their heads.

Then, as I mused about all these mighty prehistoric beasts, I found myself slipping in my imagination backwards to the ages when there was no life on the earth at all; and even further back, to the time when the whole universe was in a state of flux. I felt that the earth was a mass of white-hot gas, as large and brilliant as the sun itself. I felt myself gliding through outer space, till even my body seemed to be no more than a stream of vapour in the orbit of some flaming satellite.

What a strange dream! I was no longer aware of my uncle, the guide, or the raft; I was in a sort of cosmic trance.

'Axel!' My uncle's voice roused me. I was so close to the edge of the raft that I would have fallen overboard if Hans had not gripped me tight with his strong hand. I looked up at my uncle with unseeing eyes.

'What's the matter? Are you sick, or out of your wits?' he said.

'No . . .' I was rubbing my eyes. 'I . . . I had a sort of dream. . . . Are we all right?'

'Quite all right! A fair breeze, a calm sea – we can't be far from land.'

I sat up and looked at the horizon, but I could see nothing but water and clouds.

32

A Battle of Monsters

Saturday, 15th August. Still the same empty sea, the circle of the horizon seemed a very long way away. My head was still heavy from my strange day-dream.

My uncle had had no dreams, but he was in a bad temper. He kept on looking all round the horizon with a frustrated air. I wondered what was worrying him; our voyage was going very well indeed.

'What's the matter, Uncle?' I asked. 'You seem anxious.'

'Not at all,' he answered shortly.

'Impatient, then.'

'Why not? It's a free country, I hope?'

'But we're moving very fast . . .'

'What of that? Our speed is not too little, but the sea's far too big!' He had estimated the sea to be about a hundred miles across, but we had voyaged for three hundred miles and there was still no sight of land to the south.

'We're not getting *down*!' he went on. 'This is nothing but sheer waste of time; I haven't come so far to go for a pleasure-cruise on a pond!'

'But,' I said, 'so long as we're on Saknussemm's route . . .'

'That's the whole point. Are we on Saknussemm's route? Did he cross this water? That stream we took for guide, hasn't it led us astray?'

'But surely you can't be sorry we came this way. The sights we've seen . . .'

'Sights! What do I care for sights? I have an object, and I intend to succeed in it! Don't talk to me of sights!'

I retired into my shell, while the professor lapsed into a gloomy silence. At six o'clock in the evening Hans claimed his wages, and his three rixdollars were handed to him.

Sunday, 16th August. Nothing new. The weather was the same, the wind slightly stronger. The light was as bright as ever. The sea seemed to be infinite – as big as the Mediterranean, or even the Atlantic. And why not, indeed?

My uncle tried to take soundings. He tied one of the heaviest picks to the end of a rope four hundred yards long. It did not touch bottom and we had difficulty in hauling in our line. When at last we recovered the pick, Hans pointed out a row of deep dents, as if the iron had been gripped in a rough vice. I looked at Hans.

'*Tander!*' he said. I did not understand, and looked towards my uncle. But he was in a brown study and I did not want to disturb him. I turned to Hans again. He opened and closed his jaws, and I understood.

'Teeth!' I cried, looking at the iron bar again. Yes, the dents were certainly teeth-marks, but what prodigious beast could have made them? Some ancient monster, fiercer than a shark, more formidable than a killer-whale! I could not take my eyes from the gnawed iron. Was my dream about to become reality? These thoughts weighed on my mind and troubled my sleep.

Monday, 17th August. I started thinking about prehistoric reptiles, trying to recall what I knew about their individual characteristics. They had been in complete command of the seas; they were gigantic and terribly powerful. Our modern alligators and crocodiles, however nasty to meet, would be child's play compared with their ancestors.

I shuddered. I had seen the skeleton of one of these saurians in the Hamburg Museum; it was at least thirty feet long. Was it to be our fate to meet one of these creatures in the living flesh? It seemed impossible; but then I had another look at the iron bar, and there were the terrible marks plain to be seen.

I looked in terror at the sea. My uncle must have shared my thoughts, if not my fears, for he too, after examining the pick, was gazing out over the water.

'What could have possessed him to take soundings?' I thought. 'He's wakened one of these monsters from its age-long sleep, and now it'll be on the warpath!' I took a look at the guns; they were loaded and ready, my uncle saw what I was doing and nodded his approval.

I was right! I could see an eddying on the surface; something was moving not far away.

Tuesday, 18th August. Evening came, or rather the time to sleep, for there was no night in this ocean, and the cruel light was a weariness to the eyes. Hans was at the tiller: during his watch I fell asleep.

I was wakened by a violent shock; the raft was lifted bodily from the sea and hurled to a great distance; by extraordinary good fortune it was not upset.

'What is it?' said my uncle, still half asleep. 'Have we run aground?'

Hans was pointing with his finger; we saw a dark mass rising and falling in the sea, about five hundred yards away.

'An enormous porpoise!' I cried.

'Yes,' my uncle shouted, 'and now I can see an uncommonly large lizard!'

'And over there – see – a monstrous crocodile! Look at its great jaws filled with rows of teeth! It's diving!'

'A whale!' cried the professor. 'Look at its flippers – and now it's blowing!'

Two great water-jets rose high into the air. We were paralysed with fear. All these sea-monsters at once! – and the smallest of them could shatter the raft with one snap of its jaws or lash of its mighty tail. Hans came to his senses and started to put the tiller hard over, when we saw yet more enemies on the other beam – a turtle forty feet across, and a serpent thirty feet long, darting its huge head here and there above the waves.

We were cut off. They were drawing near, sweeping round the raft faster than the fastest convoy, making huge rings in the water. I took my gun. But what impression could a bullet make against these armour-plated brutes?

We were dumb with terror. They were coming near, to starboard the crocodile, to port the serpent. The other creatures seemed to have vanished. I was about to fire, when Hans stopped me. The two monsters passed us, a hundred yards away, hurling themselves against one another with such frenzy that they did not notice the raft.

135

Then began an epic fight; we had a ringside seat.

It seemed to me that the other beasts were now taking part in the fight, the porpoise, the whale, the lizard, the turtle – I kept on seeing parts of all of them. I pointed them out to the Icelander, but he only shook his head.

'*Tva*,' he said.

'Only two! He thinks there are only two!'

'He's right,' cried my uncle, 'he's been looking through the telescope all the time.'

'Are there really only two?'

'Yes! The first has the snout of a porpoise, the head of a lizard, and the teeth of a crocodile – that's why we were bewildered. It's the most alarming of the antediluvian reptiles – the Ichthyosaurus!'

'What about the other?'

'That's the serpent with the shell of a turtle – the Plesiosaurus!'

Now I could see that there were indeed only two monsters. I saw the bloodshot eye of the Ichthyosaurus, as big as a man's head. The whole creature was at least a hundred feet long, as I could judge when its vertical tail-fins came up out of the water. Its huge jaws had at least a hundred and eighty-two teeth, according to the naturalists.

The Plesiosaurus was a sort of sea-serpent with a short tail and legs sticking out like oars. Its body was covered with a shell, and its neck swayed about like a swan's, towering thirty feet above the waves.

These beasts were now locked in a life-and-death struggle; the violent contortions of their bodies caused mountainous seas which tossed the raft about like a cork. Twenty times we were on the point of overturning. Violent hissing like steam–whistles pierced our ears.

For an hour we watched the furious fight, and still another hour passed without a decision. The battle swayed towards the raft, then away again. We clung on as best we could, our guns loaded, unable to tear ourselves away from the scene of this stupendous struggle.

Suddenly both monsters disappeared below the waves, down the gulf of a mighty whirlpool they had made in their rage. I wondered whether the fight would go on under water.

Then all at once a huge head was thrust up from the sea, the head of the Plesiosaurus. The monster was mortally wounded, only its head and long neck were visible above the waves. The neck twisted this way and that in violent contortions, lashing the foaming water like a giant whip, wriggling like a severed worm. Water dashed upwards, blinding us, but it was almost the end of the death-agony. The reptile's convulsions slackened, and soon its long serpent's body lay still on the calmed waves.

We wondered whether the Ichthyosaurus had gone to lick its wounds in its submarine cavern, or whether it was about to emerge again and turn its fury against us poor humans on our defenceless raft.

33

Axel Island

Wednesday, 19th August. A happy wind blew us quickly from the battle-field. Hans was still at the helm. My uncle, roused for a time from his obsession by the excitement of the fight, had now sunk back into his impatient scanning of the sea.

Thursday, 20th August. Wind N.N.E., variable. Hot weather. Our speed was about nine knots.

About noon I began to hear a distant noise, like a continuous roar.

'There must be some rock or island,' said the professor.

Hans climbed the mast, but could see nothing.

Three hours later the noise was louder. It sounded to me like water falling. I wondered whether we were heading for some cataract which would dash us down into the abyss. This might do very well for the professor, who delighted in the vertical, but I was not so keen.

The roaring had now become very loud. I wondered whether it came from the sky or the sea. I looked upwards, trying to see through the clouds, but they were high and still, shining in the radiant light.

I scanned the sea again. If the whole mass of the ocean were making towards some cataract, then there ought to be a current. I threw an empty bottle overboard, but it stayed where I had thrown it. There was no current.

About four o'clock, Hans climbed the mast again. He scanned the wide arc of the sea ahead, then his eyes became fixed on one point. He dropped to deck again, and pointing to the south, he said:

'*Der nere!*'

'Down there!' said my uncle. He seized the telescope, and looked through it for a long minute. 'Yes! Yes!' he said.

'What is it?'

'A huge jet of water shooting up from the sea.'

'Another sea-monster?'

'Perhaps.'

'Then for pity's sake let's steer clear of it!' I pleaded.

'Straight ahead!' said my crazy uncle.

I turned towards Hans, who held the tiller as steady as a rock. As we drew nearer, the column of water looked higher. What terrible monster could be spouting water to such a height?

At eight in the evening we were about five miles away. A huge dark body lay full length on the sea like an island. I wondered if I was seeing things. It seemed to be two thousand yards long! Some monstrous prehistoric whale lay silent, asleep on the waves which broke against its mountainous flanks. The column of water, shooting five hundred feet into the air, fell down again with a deafening sound. We were rushing head-long, like the Gadarene swine, towards this leviathan which could easily swallow a hundred whales a day and still be hungry.

I was overcome with fear. I was not going to run to my death like a maniac! If necessary I would cut the halyard which held the sail, I would stage a one-man mutiny.

Suddenly Hans rose to his feet, and pointed to the monster.

'*Holm!*' he said.

'An island!' said the professor, roaring with laughter.

'But what about the waterspout?' I muttered helplessly.

'*Geysir!*' said Hans.

'Of course, that's what it is,' said my uncle. 'A geyser – like those in Iceland!'

I was abashed. No monster of supernatural size, nothing but an island after all – it was certainly a great relief. As we drew nearer I saw that the island was indeed shaped very like a whale, with the geyser spouting out at one end, as if from the head.

'Let's have a look at this island,' said the professor.

We had to steer clear of the geyser, which would have sunk the raft. Hans made for the other end, and brought us close in shore.

I jumped to land, my uncle followed, but Hans stayed at his post with godlike detachment; he was above our vulgar curiosity.

The granite soil was burning hot. We came to the pool from which the geyser rose, it was boiling like a witch's cauldron. I plunged in a thermometer which registered one hundred and sixty-three degrees Centigrade.[1]

So there was a central furnace after all! I pointed this out to my uncle, but he was not in the least put out. I was sure that

[1] 325°F.

we should finally arrive at a point where we should be driven back by intolerable heat, in spite of his obstinacy.

He baptised this volcanic island with my name. I was not at all sure whether this was a compliment.

We returned to the raft and jumped on board; Hans had been spending the time putting everything shipshape.

Before we cast off, I took several observations, which I noted in my log. We had sailed eight hundred and ten miles from Port Gretel, and we were now 1860 miles from Iceland, under England.

34

Storm at Sea

Friday, 21st August. Next day we were out of sight and sound of Axel Island with its geyser. A strong wind sprang up and there was a change in the weather.

The atmosphere became highly charged with electricity. The clouds had come down low and darkened to an olive hue, so that they shut out most of the light. My head ached heavily as always before a thunderstorm; the dark masses of the cumulus clouds heaped up on the southern horizon looked fierce and threatening. The wind dropped and the air weighed on the sea, now ominously calm.

The air was saturated with electricity; I could feel my hair standing up on my scalp. By ten o'clock in the morning it looked as if the storm was about to break, and I spoke of it to the professor.

He did not answer. He was in a murderous mood, because of the endlessness of the sea.

'We'll have a storm,' I repeated. 'Look at those clouds!'

Still he said nothing and a deathly silence held the whole

scene. The raft was motionless on the level water, the sail hung limp.

'Let's lower the mast and take down the sail,' I said. 'Surely that would be safest?'

'No!' cried my uncle, shaking his fist at the sky, 'hell, no! Let the wind catch us up – let the storm take us! I'll reach the shore by hook or by crook, I'll dash the raft to pieces against the rocks, as long as we get to the end of this cursed sea!'

He spoke, and at once a hurricane sprang up on the southern horizon. We could see the distant rain lashing down, while the darkness deepened. The raft bounded beneath us like a live thing; my uncle lost his balance and fell flat. When I crawled towards him, I found he was clinging to the end of a cable and staring with delighted eyes at the fury of the elements.

Hans stayed as still as a statue. His long hair, blown by the wind across his impassive face, was alive with sparks; he looked like a prehistoric man, contemporary of the dinosaur.

The mast was still in position, though it creaked at the joints, and the sail was swollen like a bubble on the point of bursting. The raft fled madly before the wind.

'The sail! The sail!' I cried, making signs to haul it down.

'No!' my uncle shrieked.

'*Nej!*' said Hans, shaking his head very slightly.

The rain was a roaring cataract between us and the horizon towards which we were dashing like maniacs. But before we reached the rain, the blanket of cloud was rent, the sea boiled and the storm burst in ear-splitting thunder over our heads. Lightning flashed round us in dazzling streams, the mass of the vapours became incandescent, the hailstones glowed as if they were on fire when they struck the metal of our tools and our guns, each crest of the raging sea was crowned with flame.

My eyes were dazzled by the intensity of the light, my ears ached with the repeated thunder-claps; I clung to the mast, which was bending like a reed under the wind . . .

Sunday, 23rd August. A terrible night; the storm was still raging in the morning. The din did not slacken for an instant; our ears were bleeding; we could not exchange a word.

Forked lightning zigzagged continuously between the water and the granite vault; I felt that the vault might split. Balls of fire formed in the air and burst like bombs. The noise was indescribable, it had passed the limits of human hearing; if all the dynamite in the world were to blow up at once the noise could not be louder.

Where were we going? My uncle lay full length on the end of the raft. It was terribly hot . . . it was like being at the mouth of a blast-furnace . . .

Monday, 24th August. There was no end to the storm. Only Hans seemed completely unaffected.

At noon the violence of the hurricane became even greater; we lashed ourselves to the raft; the waves rose over our heads. For three days we had not been able even to hear ourselves speak. My uncle put his mouth to my ear and tried to say something; I believe he said, 'We are lost,' but I could not be sure. I took a pencil and scribbled, as well as I could, 'Haul in the sail,' and he nodded.

Suddenly a ball of fire appeared at the edge of the raft. At the same time the mast and the sail were torn away; I watched them whirling up to a fantastic height.

We were paralysed with fear; the fireball, half white, half blue, as big as a football, hovered, moving slowly sideways, but spinning like a top under the lash of the hurricane. It wandered about – rolled up on to one of the joints of the raft – jumped to a bag of food – glided slowly down – leapt up again, skimming over the case of gunpowder – we stared in horror, waiting for the explosion – no – it wandered away again. Now it came close to Hans who gazed at it, then rolled towards my uncle who started back, then it came in my direction. It twirled beside my foot; I tried to draw it back but it was stuck, I could not move it. There was a stifling smell of nitrous gas.

It was horrifying not to be able to move my foot. I realised that the fireball had magnetised all the iron on board; the tools and instruments had locked together with clicking sounds; the nails in my boot were glued to a piece of iron sunk in the deck.

By a violent effort I managed to pull my foot away just before the ball touched it.

Suddenly the fireball exploded in a flare of blue–white light; we were covered with jets of flame.

Then just as suddenly the fire went out; I had time to catch a glimpse of my uncle lying on deck, and Hans always at his tiller, spitting fire like a dragon!

Where were we bound . . . ?

Tuesday, 25th August. I came gradually to my senses again after a fainting-fit which must have lasted a very long time. The storm was still raging; lightning was still running through the sky like a brood of fiery serpents with forked tongues.

We were still on the sea; still scudding with terrific speed in spite of the loss of the sail. Where could we be now? We must

have passed under England and France, under the whole of
Europe perhaps . . .

We heard a new sort of noise, something we had not yet
heard in all this devil's concert . . . the sound of surf breaking
on the rocks . . .

35

The Compass

My log of the voyage was saved from the shipwreck, by some miracle.

I cannot give a clear account of the wreck itself. I know that I felt myself in the sea, and that I was saved from drowning or from being dashed to pieces on the rocks by the strong arm of Hans. He carried me beyond the reach of the waves and laid me on the burning sand, where I found myself side by side with my uncle.

Then he went back to save what he could from the wreck. I lay in utter exhaustion. The rain was still falling in a steady downpour, though we were a little sheltered from it by overhanging rocks. Hans prepared some food; I myself could eat nothing, and soon we sank into an uneasy slumber.

Next day the weather was glorious; the sky and the sea were at peace after the terrible storm. I was awakened by joyful cries from my uncle.

'Well, my boy, how have you slept?'

'All right, thanks. You seem very cheerful.'

'Happy! I'm so happy! Here we are at last!'

'This is the end of our expedition, then?'

'Not at all, but the end of that terrible sea! Now at last we can go *down* again, now we can really find the centre of the earth!'

My heart sank. 'But, Uncle . . .'

'Well, what?'

'How shall we ever get back again?'

'Oh, Axel! You think of nothing but that. What a feeble chap you are! But you'll find it will be so easy; as soon as we reach the centre, we shall either find a new way up again, or return by the path we came; not very interesting but it will serve, at a pinch. I don't suppose it will have closed up.'

I was resigned to my fate. 'Then we'll have to repair the raft.'

'Of course.'

'What about our food?'

'I think we'll find that Hans has saved most of the cargo, he's a very resourceful fellow. Let's go and see.'

We made our way down to the beach. I was half hoping, and at the same time fearing, that the raft had been shattered to atoms with all its cargo. But there was Hans in the middle of a crowd of objects arranged neatly in piles. My uncle slapped him on the back, and pressed his hand to show his gratitude. The guide had been toiling all night while we slept; with extraordinary devotion he had saved our most precious possessions at the risk of his life.

Of course we had lost a good deal, including our guns. The case of gunpowder was, however, intact – though it had nearly blown us all up in the storm. The professor started going through the salvaged stores.

'Here's the manometer – that's worth the rest of the

instruments put together!' he said. 'With this, I can calculate the depth and know when we've reached the centre. Without it we might very likely go right through and come out in Australia!'

His brand of humour did not appeal to me. 'What about the compass?' I asked.

'Here it is, on this rock, in perfect condition, as well as the chronometer and the thermometers. Hans has done very well.'

All the instruments had been saved, and the sand was littered with ladders, cords, picks, axes, etc.

'How about the provisions?' I asked.

We looked through the pile. The cases containing the foodstuffs had mostly survived intact; the professor estimated that we still had enough for four months.

'In four months,' he said, 'we've plenty of time to complete our trip and get back to Hamburg, and with what's left over I shall give a celebration banquet to my scientific colleagues!'

I ought to have been used to my uncle by now, but he still had the power of stunning me with his colossal optimism.

'Now,' he went on, 'look at all these hollows in the rocks full of good fresh rainwater; we'll stock up at once. And I'll set Hans to work at repairing the raft, though I don't suppose we'll need it. Let's have some breakfast.'

We climbed up to the place where Hans had prepared the meal on a high rock, and ate an excellent breakfast of dried meat, biscuit and hot tea. It was the most welcome food I had ever tasted.

Over the meal we tried to work out our position. The storm had upset all our calculations, but at a rough estimate, we came to the conclusion that we must be somewhere under the

Mediterranean or its surrounding countries. We were certain that the direction of the wind had remained more or less constant, and we guessed that the beach where we were now encamped lay to the south-east of Port Gretel, where we had first embarked. We decided to consult the compass, to make sure.

So my uncle ran off gaily to look at the instrument on the rock where it lay. He set it carefully on a horizontal place, waited for the needle to settle, and looked. He rubbed his eyes and took another look. Then he came back to my side, with a white and haggard face.

'What's the matter?' I asked in alarm.

He handed the compass to me in silence. I laid it flat and looked. The north point of the needle set towards the land, not the sea! It was the exact opposite of what we had thought. I shook the compass and examined it; it was in perfect condition. The needle pointed inflexibly towards the land.

The wind must have veered right round during the storm, and hurled us back on the same shore from which we had first sailed.

36

A Human Skull!

It would be impossible to describe my uncle's feelings. From absolute stupefaction and disbelief, he came at last to furious anger. He started cursing his fate, which he felt had been playing a monstrous game of snakes-and-ladders with him, so that instead of finding himself at the foot of a ladder he was now at the tail-end of a snake. But he was determined not to give in; he stood up high on the rock waving his arms and defying fate like a champion of old.

This was too much for me. I started lecturing him, very calmly, trying to make him give up his mad resolve. I pointed out that it was a miracle that we had come safely through the storm, and that it would be tempting providence to set sail again on our frail raft. I went on like this for a long time, but he took not the slightest notice – in fact, I do not think he even heard me. At last I stopped for lack of breath, and all he said was:

'To the raft!'

By then, Hans had finished his repairs; already the rents were sealed and a new sail was flapping at a new mast. The professor spoke to Hans, who started carrying our stores on board again and stowing them ready for departure.

There was no help for it. I was one against two, and I had no hopes of breaking down the guide's feudal allegiance to his master. So I went towards the raft like a prisoner walking the plank.

But my uncle held me back.

'Not today,' he said. 'We'll start tomorrow. As we are here, I'd like to explore this new part of the coast.'

The country here was indeed quite different from the neighbourhood of Port Gretel.

'Let's explore, then,' I said cheerfully, reprieved for a day at least.

We left Hans to his own devices, and set off. The cliffs stood a great way back from the sea. In between was a vast stretch of sand covered with a multitude of shells of all sorts and sizes, from the tiniest, to gigantic turtle shells of fifteen feet across.

After walking along this sandy beach for about a mile we came to a rocky place, where we had to make our way with difficulty over great steep slabs of granite, streaked with flint and quartz. Beyond the rocks was a vast plain covered with bones, stretching away to the distant horizon. For miles we walked with our feet crunching the remains of prehistoric animals, enough to stock all the natural history museums of the world. My uncle was filled with rapturous delight at the sight of so much material for scientific study; it was almost too much for him.

Suddenly he stooped and picked up something from the ground.

'Axel!' he called, in a trembling voice, 'a human skull!'

You will be able to understand his excitement when I remind you that at this time the whole scientific world was in a fever over the discovery in 1863 of a fossil human jawbone near Abbeville in France. This was the first fossil of the kind to be excavated; it lay at a depth of fourteen feet and was surrounded by stone axes and worked flints, evidently of the same date. There had been a tumult of argument over this fossil jawbone – whether it was genuine or a carefully contrived fake – and all the most famous archaeologists of France, England and Germany, including Professor Lidenbrock, had thrown themselves into the fray on one side or the other. My uncle, of course, was quite certain that it was genuine, and now with the discovery of this complete skull he was convinced that he had been proved right.

But a yet greater thrill was in store for us. Not twenty paces from the skull, we found ourselves face to face with a complete prehistoric man, a recognisable human body.

We know that complete bodies of ancient men have been preserved in the peat-bogs of northern Europe. No doubt some such strange peculiarity of the soil here had mummified the corpse we saw before us now. The stretched skin looked like parchment, the teeth were intact, the hair was abundant and the finger- and toe-nails very long.

I stood dumb before this apparition from another age. Even my uncle, seldom at a loss for words, was silent. We lifted the body and set it upright against a rock, where it stared at us from its hollow eye-sockets.

My uncle recovered himself. Never in all his career as a university professor had he been presented with such a magnificent subject for a lecture! He could not contain himself, but launched into a flood of oratory, addressing an imaginary audience. It was very entertaining, and he certainly rose to the occasion. It was a pity that I was his only auditor.

When at last he came to an end, I clapped my hands, the only living person to applaud him in this graveyard of the ancient dead. For this body was not the only one. We found many others as we advanced along the shore.

One question tormented us. Had these men and beasts slipped down from the earth's surface to their present resting-place as a result of some convulsion of the ground? Or had they lived in this underground world, being born and dying here like the inhabitants of the upper earth? Until now, the only living creatures we had seen were fishes and sea-monsters. Were we to come face to face with a living human being on these desolate shores?

37

The Dagger of Saknussemm

We were not yet at the end of the field of bones. I was wondering whether we had come to the limit of the marvels of the cavern, or whether it still held some new wonder for our discovery.

The sea-shore disappeared behind the bone-strewn hills. The professor led me on and on, as if it did not occur to him that we might easily lose our way. It was very light, for the electric rays were diffused and shone equally on all sides of objects so that there were no shadows.

At last we came in sight of a huge forest, not like the mushroom wood we had seen before. Here was the magnificent vegetation of the Tertiary period: great palm-trees of extinct species, pines, yews, cypress and thuya, linked together by a tangled mass of creepers. The ground was carpeted with moss and plants. Streams murmured under the trees – not in the shade, since there was no shade. On their banks grew luxuriant tree-ferns like hot-house plants. But there was no colour in these trees and bushes, growing as they did without sunlight. They were all of a faded grey like a landscape in a dream or under moonlight. Even the flowers had neither colour nor scent, but seemed to be made of bleached paper.

The professor ventured under the towering trees. I followed him uneasily; the wood was full of the sort of plants that grazing animals love to feed on; it was all too likely that we should meet some of those formidable prehistoric mammals. All the trees of the world were mingled here, the oak grew beside the palm, the gum-tree close to the pine, the kauri of New Zealand mingled its branches with the northern birch.

Suddenly I stopped dead, gripping my uncle's arm.

The pervading light made it possible to see the slightest details in the surrounding thickets. I thought I saw . . . no! . . . I really *did* see, with my very eyes, mighty forms moving under the trees. There, apparent to our modern sight, was a herd of Mammoth, not fossil but alive! I saw these colossal elephants with their huge trunks swarming under the trees like a legion of serpents. I heard the noise of their long ivory tusks tearing the bark of the ancient tree-trunks. Branches crackled, leaves rustled as they were torn off and devoured by the mighty jaws of the monsters.

My day-dream on the raft had become reality. There we were, at the mercy of these ferocious beasts of the prehistoric world. My uncle was gazing in rapture.

'Come along,' he said, dragging me forward by the arm, 'let's have a good look!'

'No! No!' I cried, 'we're unarmed, they'll trample us to death! No human being could stand up against them!'

'No human being!' said my uncle, lowering his voice. 'You're wrong, Axel – look over there! I think I can see a human being – a *man*!'

I looked, incredulous. But there, less than a quarter of a mile away, leaning against the trunk of an enormous kauri-tree, was a mighty man. A giant herdsman kept watch over the Mammoths, a monster twelve feet tall. His head was as big as a buffalo's, his tangled hair was like a lion's mane. In his hand he brandished a young tree, a fitting crook for this prehistoric shepherd.

We stood paralysed with amazement. At any moment we might be seen.

'For goodness' sake let's get out of here!' I whispered, pulling at my uncle's arm. For the first time he gave way to me, and soon we were out of sight of the giant herdsman.

Now that I can think quietly, months after the event, I wonder whether our eyes were not deceived. Could it really have been a man? Was it not rather some specimen of a giant ape, larger than any that has yet been discovered in the form of fossil remains? Surely an ape, never a man!

But at the time, we fled in panic from the luminous forest, overwhelmed by our fears. It was a real race, but it felt like one of those terrifying nightmares.

Instinctively we made our way back towards the sea. Although I was sure we had never been that way before, I began to have the feeling that I had already seen some of these rock formations. They reminded me vividly of the neighbourhood of Port Gretel, and I began to think that we should soon arrive at the cavern into which I had tumbled half dead, and find our faithful Hansbrook again. The professor appeared to share my thoughts.

'It seems to me,' I said at last, 'that if we go a little further along the shore here, we'll come to Port Gretel.'

'In that case,' said the professor, 'we'd much better return straight away to the raft. But are you sure, Axel?'

'It's difficult to be sure, when all these rocks look alike. But I really think that this is the place where Hans built the raft — we ought to be quite close to the harbour — if perhaps this isn't the harbour itself . . .' I was gazing at a little creek which I thought I recognised.

'Then we ought to find some traces of our occupation, but I can't see anything . . .'

'But I can!' I shouted, running towards an object lying on the sand.

'What's that you've got?' I showed him the dagger I had just picked up. 'Is this yours?' he asked.

'No, isn't it yours?' He shook his head. 'Then it must belong to Hans.'

'I'm sure it never was his,' said my uncle, examining the weapon. 'Axel, this is a sixteenth-century dagger, a Spanish blade, of the kind worn by noblemen in their belts to guard against sudden attack; it belongs neither to you, nor to me, nor to the guide!'

'You mean . . .'

'Look — these notches — they were never made by the flesh of foes — and this coat of rust — it's the rust of centuries!' He was carried away by the strength of his imagination. 'Axel,' he went on, 'we're on the edge of a great discovery! This dagger has been lying on the sand for three hundred years, its blade was notched on the rocks of this subterranean sea!'

'Then someone has been this way before . . .'

'Yes, a man — a man who carved his name with this dagger! A man who wanted once again to blaze the trail to the centre of the earth! We must find his mark!'

In desperate excitement we started looking along the high wall of the cliff, searching for the slightest crack which might prove to be the doorway to a tunnel. We came at last to a place where the beach narrowed: the sea came almost to the foot of the cliffs, leaving a strip of sand only about six feet wide. Between two projecting rocks we saw the entrance to a dark passage. There, on a granite slab, we made out two runic letters almost eaten away by time; the initials of the bold, fantastic traveller:

$$\cdot \; \mathbf{4} \; \cdot \; \mathbf{4} \; \cdot$$

'A.S.!' cried my uncle. 'Arne Saknussemm! Arne Saknussemm again!'

38

An Obstacle

Since our voyage began, I had seen so many strange and marvellous things that I would have thought I had lost the power of wonder. But at the sight of these initials, carved three hundred years before, I fell into an ecstasy of amazement. Not only was the signature of the alchemist before my eyes, but the very dagger he had used to carve it was in my hands. My last faint doubts about Saknussemm and his voyage were overcome. My uncle was delighted and launched off into a long tirade in praise of his hero. Then he named the point of land Cape Saknussemm.

I was caught up whole-heartedly in my uncle's enthusiasm and forgot all my former fears.

'Come on!' I cried, 'what are we waiting for?' and I leapt towards the dark mouth of the tunnel. But the professor stopped me; it was his turn to be patient, while I was eaten up with impatience.

'First we'll go back and find Hans,' he said, 'and bring the raft along to this place.'

'Haven't we been astonishingly lucky, Uncle,' I said, as we

made our way back along the coast. 'If it hadn't been for that storm which hurled us back to the northern shore of the sea, we should never have come upon Saknussemm's trail!'

'Yes,' said my uncle, 'it's an extraordinary piece of luck, as you say, that we should have landed in the north when we were sailing southwards, and I still can't understand it at all.'

'Never mind,' I said, 'what does it matter, so long as we've found the right way?'

'It's all turned out for the best, and at last we're leaving this horizontal sea behind. We'll go down, down, down! We're only a little more than 4000 miles from the centre now!'

'What's 4000 miles?' I said. 'Hardly worth mentioning!'

We were a pair of maniacs now. With such crazy talk we passed the time till we found the guide again. All was ready for an immediate start; the baggage was stowed and the sail ready to hoist. We went on board, Hans took the tiller, and we sailed along the coast towards Cape Saknussemm.

It was not easy to steer our unmanageable craft so close to the shore. Sometimes we had to punt ourselves along with poles, and sometimes we had to make wide detours to avoid reefs. At last, after a three-hour trip – that is to say, about six in the evening – we found a good place to tie up, close to the entrance of the tunnel.

I jumped ashore, followed by my uncle and the Icelander. I was still as eager as before, and even proposed to burn our boat, in the traditional heroic style, to cut off all possibility of retreat. My uncle, however, was half-hearted about the idea.

'At least,' I said, 'let's start this very minute!'

'Yes, of course, my dear boy, but first, let's have a look at this new gallery, in case we need our ropes.'

He switched on his Ruhmkorff lamp. We left the raft moored to the rocks and made for the mouth of the tunnel, which was only twenty paces away. I was in the lead.

The entrance was almost circular and about five feet across, the bottom of the hole just touching the ground. The dark tunnel was glazed inside by the action of the molten lava which had once burst through it. The passage was almost level, but I had not taken six steps when I was stopped by a huge block of stone.

I was furious at the sudden end to the new path. We looked to right and to left, up and down, but there was no other passage. Hans shone the lamp all over the walls, I scrabbled about at the foot of the block, but it was a dead end.

I sank down to the floor, while my uncle paced the corridor.

'What about Saknussemm?' I cried.

'Yes, what indeed?' said my uncle. 'Was he locked out by this stone door?'

'No, surely not,' I answered. 'This rock must have fallen and blocked the way long after Saknussemm's time. Surely we can force our way through?'

My uncle looked at me with some astonishment; was this his timorous nephew?

'We can have a go with the pick,' he suggested.

'It's too hard,' I said, 'it would take far too long.'

'Well, then?' He was looking to me for suggestions!

'Let's blast our way through!' I said. 'It's nothing but a bit of rock.'

The professor spoke to Hans, who went to the raft and fetched a pick. Then he began to hack out a hole in which to set the explosive charge. This was no mean task; the hole had to be long enough to take fifty pounds of gun-cotton.

I was terribly excited. I tried to keep calm while Hans worked by helping my uncle make a fuse from damp gun-powder packed into a linen tube.

'We'll get through!' I said.

'So we will!' my uncle agreed.

By midnight our mine was complete. The charge was packed in position, and the long fuse reached just outside the entrance to the tunnel. A spark would set it off.

'Till tomorrow!' said the professor.

Six long hours to wait!

39

Into the Abyss

Next day, Thursday, 27th August, was a famous date. Even now I cannot think of it without horror. From that day, we lost control of our fate, and became the playthings of natural forces.

By six in the morning we were up. I begged for the honour of springing the mine. Hans and my uncle were to board the raft, which was still loaded with our stores, and I was to run and join them when I had lit the fuse. Then we would push off as far as possible from the shore and await results.

The fuse was timed to burn for ten minutes, so we should have plenty of time, if all went according to plan.

We made a hasty meal, and the others embarked. I held a lighted lantern in my hand.

'Good luck, my boy,' said the professor, 'don't hang about!'

'I shan't,' I said firmly. I went to the mouth of the tunnel, took the end of the fuse, and opened the lantern.

The professor was watching his chronometer.

'Ready?' he called.

'Yes, ready!'

'Let her go!'

I held the fuse in the flame, it caught and started spluttering. I ran to the water and jumped aboard; Hans pushed off with a strong thrust of his pole. The raft drifted out from the shore.

It was a nerve-racking moment. The professor watched the hand of the chronometer.

'Five more minutes!' he said. 'Now four . . . three . . .' My pulse beat the seconds. 'Two . . . one! Fall, granite mountains!'

What happened then? I was hardly aware of the noise of the detonation; but the form of the rocks suddenly changed, opening like a curtain before my eyes. A vast abyss yawned in the middle of the beach. The dizzy sea became one enormous wave: our raft stood up on end and we were thrown down on our faces. In the twinkling of an eye we were plunged into absolute darkness; the raft seemed to hang suspended on emptiness. I tried to speak, but the roar of the waters drowned my words.

In spite of everything I realised what had happened. Beyond the rock we had blown up had been the mouth of an abyss. The explosion had caused a sort of earthquake; the gulf had opened, and the sea was pouring down, carrying us along with it.

This was the end, I was sure.

An hour or two – how long I cannot say – passed like this. We linked arms, holding hands to prevent being thrown from the raft; every now and again it struck the wall with extreme violence. But as these shocks grew less frequent I gathered that the passage was growing wider. It was certainly Saknussemm's road, but instead of climbing quietly down, we had pulled out the bath-plug of the sea!

These thoughts whirled through my troubled brain during

our headlong rush. We seemed to be going faster than the fastest train. No lantern could be lit, and our last electric lamp had been broken by the blast of the explosion.

Suddenly to my amazement a light shone close beside me, showing up the calm face of our guide. He had managed to get the lantern lit, and though the flame fluttered wildly, it shed a little light through the hideous darkness.

The gallery was very wide, so that we could not see both walls at the same time. We were shooting rapids steeper than the wildest Red Indian would attempt; their surface seemed to be made of a bundle of liquid arrows. Sometimes the raft was caught in eddies which sent it spinning round. When we came close to the walls the bumps appeared as lines; we must have been going at least ninety miles an hour.

My uncle and I looked at each other with haggard eyes; we lay beside the stump of the mast, which had snapped off short at the moment of the catastrophe. We tried to protect our nostrils from the force of the air-stream.

Hours passed like this. I tried to arrange our cargo, and realised to my horror that most of it had disappeared. By the light of the lantern I attempted to take stock. Of our instruments, we had none but the compass and the chronometer. The ladders and ropes had been reduced to one little bit of cord wound round the stump of the mast. Not a pick, not an axe, not a hammer, and worst of all, not enough food for one day!

I dug my fingers into the crevices of the raft, the tiniest corners between the joints of the beams. Nothing! Our provisions consisted of a piece of dried meat and a few biscuits.

Of course it was silly of me to worry about our lack of food, when death faced us in so many other violent and speedy forms. But strangely enough, I still clung to our thousand-to-one chance of survival, and the loss of the food was a torment to me. But I had the self-control to spare my uncle the distress of this discovery.

At that moment, the flame in the lantern guttered and went out. We were in complete darkness, and I shut my eyes like a child to keep the darkness out.

After a long time, our speed suddenly increased, as I could feel from the air against my face. We were no longer sliding but falling. My uncle and Hans gripped me tight.

Then I felt a shock: the raft had not hit a solid object, but it had come to a dead halt. Water flooded the raft; I was suffocating – I thought I was drowning.

After a few seconds we were above the water once more, and I could breathe again. The others were holding my arms tightly, and we were all still on the raft.

40

Our Last Meal

By then it must have been about ten o'clock at night. Suddenly I found I could hear again. The roaring of the waters, which had been filling my ears for all those long hours, had ceased. There was silence in the gallery.

At last I heard my uncle's voice, very soft like a murmur: 'We're rising!'

'*What?*' I cried.

'Yes! We're rising!'

I reached out my hand and touched the wall; when I drew it back it was bleeding. We were rushing upwards.

'The lantern!' cried the professor. Hans had saved the lantern, and managed at last to re-light it. The flame flickered but did not go out; we could see our surroundings.

'It's as I thought,' said my uncle. 'We're in a narrow shaft, about twenty feet across. The water sank to the bottom of the gulf and is now rising to find its own level, and bringing us up with it.'

'But suppose there's no outlet to this shaft? We'll be crushed!' I said.

'Axel,' said the professor calmly, 'our situation is almost desperate, but we have a slight chance of escape, so I propose we renew our strength by eating.'

'Eating?' I faltered. Now I would have to tell him.

My uncle was speaking in Danish to Hans, who was shaking his head.

'What!' said the professor. 'Have we lost our food?'

I told him what we had left. He looked at me as if he did not understand, and lapsed into silence.

An hour passed. We were all beginning to feel very hungry, but none of us dared to touch the last of the food.

We were still shooting upwards; sometimes the rush of air took our breath away. At the same time, the temperature was rising, and the air becoming alarmingly hot. I had always believed in the theory of the central furnace; now it seemed as if I had been right.

'If we escape death by drowning or by being smashed to pieces,' I said, 'and if we don't starve to death, we've still got the chance of being burned alive.'

The professor shrugged his shoulders.

An hour passed. Then my uncle broke the silence.

'As I see it,' he said, 'we'd better make up our minds.'

'How do you mean?'

'We'd better share out the food and eat it. If we try to spin it out, then we shan't have the strength to save ourselves, assuming we get the chance.'

'You still have some hope, then?' I burst out in anger.

'Certainly I have. As long as my heart beats I shall never despair.' His brave words gave me a little courage.

'All right, then,' I said, 'let's eat.'

169

My uncle took the piece of meat and the few biscuits, divided them into three equal portions and shared them out. It came to about a pound of food each. The professor devoured his share with feverish haste; I ate without pleasure, almost with disgust, in spite of my hunger; Hans chewed silently, calmly, in small mouthfuls, like a man with no worries in the world. He had rummaged about and found a flask half full of gin; he passed it round, and the strong spirit cheered me.

'*Forträffig!*' said Hans as he swallowed his tot.

'Excellent!' said my uncle.

It was five in the morning. The food had revived us, but our situation was as desperate as ever. We fell to our thoughts again, which were all we had. I wondered what was in the mind of Hans, that man of the west with the resignation of an Oriental. For myself, I was thinking of home, of our house, of my poor Gretel and our dear Martha; and in the rumblings of the rock I seemed to hear the noise of the cities of the earth.

But the temperature was rising to an intolerable degree, and I was bathed in sweat. By degrees we had all taken off our coats and waistcoats. The touch of our clothes on our skin was unbearable.

'We must be rising up into a furnace!' I said.

'Nonsense,' said my uncle.

'But the wall's burning!' I was holding my hand close to it. Then my fingers skimmed the surface of the water. 'The water's boiling!' I shouted.

The professor made an angry gesture.

By the glimmering lantern I saw the walls of the shaft heaving and trembling. Some new unheard-of disaster was about to take place. I looked at the compass. It had gone mad!

170

41

The Fiery Road

The compass needle was jumping about from one point to another, twisting on its axis. At the same time, the rumblings in the shaft had swelled into thunder, making a noise like a chariot-race over cobbled streets.

'Uncle!' I cried at last, 'it's an earthquake!'

'No,' he said calmly, 'much better than that!'

'What on earth do you mean?'

'An eruption, Axel.'

'You mean – we're in the chimney of an active volcano!'

'I think so,' said the professor, smiling, 'and it's the best possible thing that could have happened!'

'What!' I cried, 'we're in the middle of an eruption! We're in a stream of white-hot lava, molten rocks, boiling water! We're to be belched out, vomited, cast up into the air with tons of rock, torrents of hot ash, in a raging whirlwind of flame! . . . And you say that's the best possible thing?'

'Yes, indeed,' said the professor, looking at me over the top of his glasses, 'since it's the only chance we have of getting back to the surface of the earth!'

I was staggered. My uncle was absolutely right, of course, but what a desperate remedy!

We were still rising, and the night passed in continuous thunder. I was almost suffocating; I felt my last hour was at hand, and yet the strangest thoughts came into my head. I began childishly wondering which volcano we could possibly be in.

It could not be Snaefells, because that was extinct. We were in the north; perhaps we were under Iceland again. I knew that Mount Hekla was still active, together with seven others in that country. Then there was the volcano called Esk, in Jan Mayen Land, not far from Spitzbergen. That might be the one. These speculations served to save my reason, I believe. Otherwise I might well have gone out of my mind.

Towards morning, our upward motion became much faster. At the same time it became even hotter. Lurid reflections began filtering through the chimney, which was growing wider; on every side I saw deep cracks belching forth clouds of smoke, while tongues of flame flickered over the rock walls.

'Look, Uncle!' I cried.

'Nothing but sulphurous flames. What could be more natural in an eruption?'

'But if they close round us?'

'They won't close round us.'

'But we shall stifle!'

'We shan't stifle, the gallery is getting wider.'

'And the water! The rising water!'

'There's no more water, Axel, but a sort of thick flow of lava which will carry us up to the mouth of the crater.'

I looked down in horror. We were indeed floating on

molten rock, bubbling furiously. It was fantastically hot, I was swimming in my sweat. If we had not been shooting up so fast we should certainly have been stifled.

About eight in the morning, the raft suddenly stopped.

'What's happened?' I cried. 'Is the eruption over?'

'I sincerely hope not,' said my uncle. He kept his eyes on his chronometer. 'Now we've been still for five minutes,' he said at last, 'we'll be moving again soon.'

As he spoke, the raft jerked upwards. It went on for about two minutes, then stopped.

'Good,' said my uncle. 'In ten minutes it will start again. This is an intermittent eruption, it gives us time to breathe.'

He was right. The raft began moving again in exactly ten minutes, in fact it shot up so fast that we had to cling on to the timbers. Then again it came to a halt.

I cannot say how many times this chain of events was repeated. Every time we moved, we were shot up violently as if from the mouth of a gun. During the moments of rest we were suffocating, and while we went upwards the burning air made it impossible to breathe. I thought with intense longing of the Arctic regions, and imagined a plain of ice and snow. I became almost unconscious, and many times the arm of Hans saved me when I was in danger of falling against the granite wall.

I have no clear memory of the hours which followed. I had a confused sensation of continuous explosions, while the whole mountain was trembling, and the raft spinning round like a top. It was floating on floods of lava, under a rain of cinders. Fierce flames licked round us, roaring up from below in a mighty updraught. I caught a glimpse of the guide's face shining against the flames, and my last conscious thought was that it must be like this to be a condemned man waiting to be shot from the mouth of a cannon.

42

Stromboli!

When I opened my eyes, I felt the strong hand of the guide clinging to my belt. With his other hand he was supporting my uncle. I seemed to be all in one piece, but I was sore and aching all over. I found myself on a mountain-side, two steps from a precipice over which I should certainly have rolled, if Hans had not saved me.

'Where are we?' muttered my uncle, who seemed to be very annoyed to find himself back on the surface of the earth. The guide shrugged his shoulders.

'In Iceland?' I ventured.

'*Nej*,' replied Hans.

'What do you mean, no?' said the professor.

'He must be wrong,' I said, sitting up.

The last surprise of this astonishing expedition was in store for us. I expected to see a cone covered with eternal snows, among the barren deserts of the north, under the pale rays of a polar sky, beyond the highest latitudes. But there we were – my uncle, the Icelander, and myself – lying halfway down a mountain scorched by the rays of the blazing sun.

I could hardly believe my eyes; but there was no mistake about the noonday heat. We had been thrown half-naked out of the crater, and the glorious sun we had not seen for two months was now lavishing its warmth and light on us.

The professor pulled himself together.

'This certainly doesn't look like Iceland!'

'I suppose it's Jan Mayen Land,' I suggested.

'I hardly think so, my dear boy. Look about you!'

Above our heads, five hundred feet away, was the crater of the volcano. Every quarter of an hour there was a thunderous explosion, and flames shot up into the sky, mingled with lava, pumice, and ashes. I could feel the trembling of the mountain as it breathed like a colossal whale, blowing fire and air through its vents. Below us was a steep slope covered with debris from the eruption. The lower slopes of the mountain were clothed in rich green trees; there were olives and fig-trees and vines laden with purple grapes.

It certainly did not look like the Arctic.

Beyond the belt of trees was the shining water of the sea, or perhaps of a great lake, which surrounded the enchanted land where we lay, and revealed it as an island only a few miles across. Below us was a little harbour-town, with ships of strange shapes riding at anchor on the blue waves. Dozens of islets dotted the distant waters. A range of blue mountains lay along the remote horizon, while further round was a high peak with a plume of smoke floating from its crest. In the opposite direction, a great expanse of water glittered under the sunlight, with here and there the tip of a mast showing or a sail swelling to the wind.

It was a gloriously beautiful scene, all the more welcome for being so unexpected.

'Where are we? Where can we be?' I murmured.

Hans shut his eyes, not caring at all, and my uncle gazed without understanding.

'Wherever we are,' he said at last, 'it's really far too hot here, and the eruption is still going on. It would be too silly to come out of a volcano alive and then be knocked on the head by a flying rock. Let's go down. Anyway, I'm dying of hunger and thirst.'

We slithered down the steep slope, crunching hot cinders, avoiding the lava streams which trickled like fiery serpents along the ground.

'We must be in Asia,' I cried, 'perhaps on the coast of India, or even in the Malay Archipelago, or Oceania!'

'What about the compass?' said my uncle.

'Oh, the compass.' I was a little put out. 'According to the compass, all the last part of our journey was towards the north.'

'Can the compass lie? Is this the north pole?'

There was no answer to the riddle. By now, however, we were drawing near to the pleasant green groves. I was desperately hungry and thirsty. After scrambling down the mountain-side for another couple of hours, we found ourselves in a delightful countryside covered with olives, pomegranate trees and vines, which seemed to belong to everyone as there were no fences. In any case we were far too hungry to care about that. We flung ourselves on the vines and pressed whole bunches of ripe grapes into our burning mouths; they tasted like the fruits of paradise. Not far away, in the cool shade of the trees, I found a spring of fresh water, where we drank eagerly and bathed our bruised and lacerated bodies.

Then we lay back, utterly content, on the grassy bank. How wonderful it was to be on earth again, to see the sky through the trees and listen to the twittering of birds!

Suddenly a little boy appeared in the olive grove.

'Happy child,' I thought, 'to live in this golden land!'

But he was a miserable, ragged little poverty-stricken creature, and he looked very frightened at the sight of us. Indeed we must have been terrifying, dirty and half-naked as we were, with great shaggy beards.

The urchin took to his heels, but Hans ran after him and brought him back, kicking and screaming. My uncle tried to reassure him, and asked him in German:

'What is this mountain called, my young friend?'

The child made no answer.

'Good,' said my uncle, 'we aren't in Germany.' So he tried English, with no better result, and afterwards French, and then Italian.

'*Dove noi siamo?*' ('Where are we?')

The child still said nothing, but he pulled a face. My uncle began to think that he was only pretending not to understand.

'*Come si noma questa isola?*' ('What is the name of this island?') he said angrily.

'Stromboli,' said the boy, wriggling out of Hans's grasp and streaking away among the olives.

Stromboli! So we were in the middle of the Mediterranean! Those blue mountains were the Calabrian Hills, on the Italian mainland, and the great volcano was Etna in Sicily! What a fantastic journey we had made, from remote Iceland and its barren deserts to this garden of the ancient world, with its delightful fruits and blue skies.

Impatiently we set off for the harbour of Stromboli. We did not think it would be wise to tell the true story of how we had arrived on the island, for the superstitious peasants would certainly think we were devils straight from hell. Our story should be that we were shipwrecked mariners. As we walked, I heard my uncle murmuring:

'But the compass! The compass pointing to the north! What *can* be the explanation?'

'Are you really still worrying about that?' I asked scornfully. 'Why don't you forget it?'

'Forget it! For a professor of Hamburg University not to find the reason for a cosmic phenomenon would be a disgrace!'

He was magnificent. I shall never forget the sight of him, as he stood there in all his professorial dignity, half-naked and with his leather money-belt round his waist, looking at me over the top of his spectacles.

We reached the harbour, and Hans claimed the wages for his twelfth week of service. My uncle gripped his hand warmly as he gave him the money. At that moment, the guide gave way to a quite unusual show of feeling – he pressed our hands lightly with the tips of his fingers and smiled.

43

The Crazy Compass

As shipwrecked seamen, we were kindly treated by the Stromboli fishermen, who provided us with food and clothing. After two days we got a passage on a local boat to Messina, where we were very glad to rest.

On Friday, 4th September, we set sail on a French mail-boat, the *Volturne*, and three days later we reached Marseilles. My uncle was still fretting about our wretched compass, but I myself did not lose much sleep over it. On the evening of 9th September we arrived at Hamburg.

Gretel and Martha were overjoyed to welcome us home safe and sound.

'You're a real hero!' Gretel whispered as I held her tight. 'Now you must never leave me again!'

The return of Professor Lidenbrock caused a sensation in Hamburg. Martha had naturally not been able to keep the secret; she had told all her friends and acquaintances that we had gone off to the centre of the earth, and so the rumour had reached the professors by way of the womenfolk. They refused to believe it – and then, when they saw him again, they still refused. But the presence of Hans, and certain news from Iceland, caused people to change their minds by degrees.

All at once my uncle became a great man, and I became the nephew of a great man – which is something, after all. The City of Hamburg gave a banquet in our honour, and the professor gave a lecture on our expedition to a vast audience in the university lecture-hall. The same day, he presented Saknussemm's manuscript to the public archives, and made a statement in which he expressed his sincere regret that circumstances beyond his control had prevented him from following the Icelander's trail to the very centre of the earth. He was modest in his glory, and his reputation gained by this.

Naturally, some scientists were jealous, and attacked him on various points of theory both to his face and in learned journals. Such controversy was meat and drink to him, and he flung himself into the battle with the greatest energy.

In the midst of all this fame and excitement, my uncle had one cause for grief: to his great sorrow, Hans insisted on leaving Hamburg. He was homesick for Iceland, and all the professor's offers could not make him change his mind.

'*Farval*' he said one day; and with this simple goodbye, he set off for Reykjavik, where he arrived after an uneventful journey. We had grown extremely attached to our brave eider-hunter, who had saved our lives so many times, and I shall certainly visit him one day before I die.

My uncle published his account of our journey, and it made the headlines throughout the world. It was translated into many languages and published in all civilised countries, besides being serialised in the most important newspapers. My uncle had the rare and happy fortune of enjoying his fame in his lifetime. He was even pressed by the great Mr Barnum to appear in his circus in America for a very high fee.

But in spite of all his glory, my uncle still suffered from a festering thorn in the flesh. It was agony for a scholar like him to have to confess himself beaten by the unexplained phenomenon of the compass.

One day, while I was arranging a collection of mineral specimens in his study, my eye fell on this famous compass. It had been lying there for six months quite quietly in its corner, with no suspicion of the excitement it had caused. I put it on the table and looked at it – then I gave a great cry. The professor came running in.

'What on earth—' he asked.

'This compass! It points to the south!'

'What!'

'Look! The poles are reversed!'

My uncle looked, then gave a jump which shook the house. A great light dawned.

'So when we reached Cape Saknussemm,' he said, 'the needle of this wretched compass was pointing to the south?'

'As you say.'

'But what could have caused this extraordinary situation?'

'You remember that fireball during the storm, when all the metal on the raft was magnetised? That must have done it.'

'*A-ha!*' he cried, with a great roar of laughter. 'So it was all a joke! An electric practical joke!'

From that day on, my uncle was the happiest of scientists, and very soon afterwards I became the happiest of men. Gretel and I were married, and she found a new uncle in Professor Otto Lidenbrock, honorary Fellow of all the scientific, geographical and mineralogical societies of the five continents.

penguin.co.uk/vintage